THE LAST KIDS ON EARTH

and the MIDNIGHT BLADE

MAX BRALLIER & DOUGLAS HOLGATE

SCHOLASTIC INC.

ISBN 978-1-338-60978-3

Text copyright © 2019 by Max Brallier. Illustrations copyright © 2019 by Douglas Holgate. All rights reserved. Published by Scholastic Inc., 557 Broadway, New York, NY 10012, by arrangement with Viking Children's Books, an imprint of Penguin Young Readers Group, a division of Penguin Random House LLC. SCHOLASTIC and associated logos are trademarks and/or registered trademarks of Scholastic Inc.

12 11 10 9 8 7 6 5 4 3 2 1   19 20 21 22 23 24

Printed in the U.S.A.   23

First Scholastic printing, September 2019

Book design by Jim Hoover
Set in Cosmiqua Com and Carrotflower

For Alyse.

For Daniels.

For Pupper.

For Everything.

—M. B.

For the "MPW Lads."

Stay savage for all time.

—D. H.

chapter one

Well, it happened. After all that time, they got us.

The zombies bit us.

We turned. We transformed.

Look at us—twisted undead faces, slumping undead posture.

We're zombies. Absolute zombies.

Quint: zombie. Dirk: zombie. June: total, big-time zombie.

Things are different now. . . .

Our adventures are a little slower: less darting around, more shambling. And our appetites have changed: less grilled donuts, more flesh burgers.

Y'know what—let me catch you up. Fill you in. Explain **HOW** we joined the ranks of the undead.

See, it's been about a month since, uh, **BIG STUFF HAPPENED**. A month since we battled a new villain; a villain who was **HUMAN**. . . .

This villain's name is **EVIE SNARK**, and like me, she's a super-mega-geek. But *unlike* me, she's OUT OF HER EVER-LOVING MIND. . . .

Out of her ever-lovin' mind.

Evil grin.

Wants to rule the end of the world.

First, she stole my beloved Louisville Slicer, and I was like, nuh-uh, NOT OK.

Then, she caused Dirk to be bitten by a zombie!

It was all part of her big bad cosmic plan—she was going to perform this weirdo ritual and bring the Cosmic Terror, **GHAZT**, into our dimension.

See, Ghazt is "The General" and he has the ability to control zombies with his **TAIL**. . . .

And that's, like, bad.

But Quint, June, and I swung in like the Three Compadres! We saved Dirk by feeding him an eyeball, lent to us by our monster buddy Warg.

The eyeball had some kind of healing, anti-zombie elixir inside, and Dirk sucked down the contents like a glass of hot, gooey lemonade. (It was gross, yep.)

We got the Slicer back, too! But not before it connected with the monster dimension. . . .

THINGS GOT WEIRD!

And in the end, well—**WE KINDA FAILED**. Evie's plan worked! Ghazt entered our dimension. But, because we interfered, things went a little sideways and Ghazt took the form of a **RAT**—a rat mixed with Evie's action figure collection. So now he's a half-plastic, half-rodent, zombie-controlling cosmic creep.

And they escaped! Evie and Ghazt: now at large, on the loose, concocting bad guy plans!

And that leads us to . . . this very morning.

And us, becoming zombies.

Me, Jack Sullivan—former Post-Apocalyptic Action Hero! Now, just a lousy Post-Apocalyptic **ZOMBIE DUDE**.

And June, Dirk, and Quint. Also zombies. We're just four, regular, normal zombies among hundreds. Things have taken a turn for the *terrifying*. . . .

"Guys, being a zombie *stinks!*" June says. "Literally. It smells."

"Don't you dare bad-mouth the smell," Quint says. "I spent weeks perfecting it!"

"Stop yappin'!" Dirk barks. "We're zombies. Zombies don't yap!"

5

OK, so . . . I lied. We're just *pretending* to be zombies. We're undercover. It's part of our top-secret *MISSION OPERATION: DEFEAT EVIE AND GHAZT!*

We are currently staggering, zombie-style, toward the Wakefield Bowl-O-Drome, which is Evie and Ghazt's villainous lair.

How do we know it's their villainous lair?

Because there are a bunch of old TVs mounted above the Bowl-O-Drome's entrance, and Evie's up there talking:

I lean over and whisper to my buddies, "Look at Evie, beckoning zombies from far and wide. She really embraced her bad side. Like full super-villain."

"It appears the zombies are drawn by her voice," Quint says.

June nods. "Yep, 'cause humans = food!"

See, we've been staking out the Bowl-O-Drome for a week, waiting for a big enough zombie horde to come along so we could slip in with them, unnoticed.

And finally they have. . . .

So we got into character and joined the walking zombie club, but not before we did a final operation checklist—Zombie makeup: Check. Gray skin, green ooze draining from our mouths, just-woke-up hair.

Zombie odor: Check. We got THE STENCH. Quint bottled it. It's awful and foul and I've got puke like three-quarters of the way up my throat—but it works.

And last but MOST IMPORTANT: the zombie walk, AKA the zombie shuffle, AKA the zombie zigzag. We knew our zombie walks had to be *perfect* if we wanted to blend in. We spent days practicing—even doing it for Bardle to make sure we had it down pat.

It all better work, because we're nearing the bowling alley entrance. There are zombies on either side of us, pressing against us. . . .

I hope Evie's ready, 'cause we're coming—and we're bringing payback! She stole my blade! Got my friend zombified! Did—just—a lot of stuff!

And *in mere moments* we're gonna hit her with that payback. All four of us, together, like the freaking Avengers. . . .

Heavy breathing—like panting—pulls me out
of my superhero squad fantasy. I expect to see a
zombie with a nasty cold, but it's actually Dirk.
And he does *not* look ready to get his Avenger on.

Which is fair. He went through some pretty
serious stuff. I mean, he's healed. But still—
upstairs—he's probably a little freaked out.

"Dirk, you OK?" I whisper.

Before he can answer, I feel a hand on mine. I look down. "June, you're holding my hand!" I whisper excitedly.

"Not holding," she says. *"Squeezing."*

"A love squeeze?"

"NO! A *hurt* squeeze," she growls through gritted teeth. "No more talking!"

June squeezes twice—extra-painful hard—and I look up as the bowling alley doors swing open.

I do my best zombie moan as we are all, together, funneled inside the villainous home base. . . .

chapter two

As soon as we're through the door, we start searching for cover. Quint silently points to a row of shelves filled with bowling shoes. Getting there is a claustrophobic nightmare—kinda feels like Best Buy on Black Friday. We're forcefully pushing ourselves through the zombie horde, trying to reach our safe place.

But we're lucky—the zombies leave us alone. The horde is morphing from a huge mushed-up mash to one organized line.

They are drawn by something we don't see or hear—and they're shuffling away from the entrance and toward the old arcade and snack bar room. When the last zombie has turned the corner, I realize that this whole place is emptier than I expected—by *a lot*. And most important— no sign of Evie or Ghazt.

Ghazt was scared of the Slicer last time, so all I gotta do is show it to him again—and he'll vamoose! But first we gotta find him.

"Guys, it's quiet," I say. *"Too quiet."*

Dirk shoots me a confused look. I see sweat pouring off his face in fat droplets.

Quiet?!

Don't you guys hear that? People, like, mumbling? Talking?

Uh . . . no?

Dirk frowns, getting sweatier, then quickly says, "Oh OK me neither just wanted to make sure."

"Guys!" Quint says in a whisper. He's using an old selfie stick with a mirror to peek around the corner. "The zombies all went into the arcade. But there are **ZOMBIE GUARDS** at the doors!"

I scooch over and glance in the mirror. I see four zombies, standing watch, wearing hooded robes. . . .

Those robes—I realize they're just like the ones we saw in Evie's book. She's drafting these zombies into her Cabal of the Cosmic!

OLD-TIMEY MEMBERS OF THE CABAL OF THE COSMIC! WAY BACK IN THE DAY.

The Cabal of the Cosmic was a group of crazy-pants people from the olden days who were *obsessed* with bad dudes like Ŗeżżóċħ the Ancient, Destructor of Worlds. Evie found their old book, full of information and instructions. (It's OK, though—we stole the book from her and now we have our *own* guide to Ŗeżżóċħ's world of cosmic horror.)

"Guys," I whisper, nodding toward the arcade snackbar, "I think that's Ghazt's *real* home base."

"A villainous lair *inside* a villainous lair?" June asks. "How many villainous lairs does one interdimensional rat monster need?"

Quint responds, "The answer, it seems, is two."

"If we're gonna sneak in and crash their evil party," I say, "we need to blend in like undercover super spies."

I lock eyes with June—and she gets it, right away. We gotta take out these guards, triple-ninja-style, and steal their dirty duds.

June nudges Quint. He pulls a whiffle ball box from his action-geek bag. But inside is no ordinary whiffle ball. Inside is the—

Whiffle Meatball
Guaranteed to get ANY zombie's attention!

Mealworms.

Jelly beans.

Rotten ham.

"I'll roll," Quint says.

"And I'll take 'em out," June adds.

With that, it's meatball away. Quint bowls it toward the arcade. It rolls past the blue-cloaked zombie guards. . . .

They look around, sniffing, then a moment later—

The guards stagger after the ball, hunched over, bony fingers grabbing and scraping. One finally collapses onto the ball, like it's trying to recover a fumble in the end zone. All four of them begin *gnawing* at the thing—*sucking* on the whiffle meatball.

Bingo. A very gross bingo.

June smiles. "I got this next part . . ." she says, and lifts her torn zombie sleeve to reveal the Gift. I got it for her this past Christmas, and it's a total monster knockout device. Also good for temporary zombie takedowns. . . .

How ya like me now?

Pop-out blade.

THWINK!

She cranks a wheel on the side, and then—

WHAFK! WHAFK! WHAFK!

Four blasts.

Four blue-robed zombies hit the floor.

We shove the zombies into a storage closet and slip into their robes. We look pretty legit!

I eye the entrance to the arcade. With the guards gone, all we have to do is slip inside. But I hesitate.

Because it's finally happening. We've searched long and hard for this foul, formidable creature that wants to rule over our broken planet. It's now or never.

I steel myself. "In we go," I whisper. "And remember: *best zombie impressions ever*. It's game time."

Hearts pounding, we push the doors open—going for total 007-level inconspicuousness, we shuffle inside.

And—well—we find the zombies, that's for sure. Hundreds of them. . . .

I'm trying to do a zombie version of "fly casual"—my face twisted to look undead, while simultaneously trying to give off a whole "Hey-how-you-doing-nice-party-come-here-often-we-totally-belong-here-and-if-you're-curious-yep-we're-definitely-zombies-no-reason-to-look-closely" vibe.

But it's hard to be casual—because what we see inside here is so bananas insane. . . .

chapter three

This lair is huge and sprawling: a combined snack bar, arcade, and bathroom.

Bits of light filter in through cracks and holes in the walls and ceiling. Vine-Thingies creep along the floor, glowing neon green and purple.

"Ghazt's not looking so hot, huh?" June whispers.

Peering through the zombie horde, I see Ghazt.

Puddle of cheese.

June's right—the general isn't exactly awe-inspiring.

In fact, Ghazt now looks more like some sort of—

LAZY TUB-O-GOO CHEESE BEAST!

"He's constructed a bed from nacho squeeze cheese," Quint remarks. "How inventive."

I'm so focused on Ghazt's transformation that it takes me a moment to notice the *weirdest* weirdness going down.

The zombies inside this strange, dark base— they're *different*.

"These robed zombies aren't just shambling about mindlessly," I whisper. "They're, like, *doing stuff.*"

What we're looking at, right now—it is mind-blasting and world-alteringly new. These zombies aren't just possessed—they're productive. . . .

At the movie theater, we saw Ghazt *move* the zombies. And we saw the zombies *carry* him. But this is more than that—these are zombie *servants*. One's even serenading Ghazt with bongo drums!

Honestly, it has the vibe of an almost cool but actually really awkward birthday party with a not-so-gracious host.

A few zombies shuffle to the side—and I spot it. The thing that we came for: Ghazt's tail. The nasty, slithering source of his zombie-controlling power. . . .

"Jack, we need to hide . . ." June whispers, tugging on my sleeve.

"This way!" Quint points to Dino Rampage—a vintage arcade game enclosed by a curtain.

We zombie-shuffle our way over—then quickly cram inside. Dino Rampage is built for two players, so the four of us are forced into an uncomfortable pile.

I feel heavy breathing on my neck—it's Dirk, huffing and sweating with claustrophobia.

And I'm feeling the way Dirk looks. We've done dangerous junk many times—but this time we're behind enemy lines, inside enemy robes! If we're not careful—this will go south before you can say "zombie bowling league."

Quint and I sneak a peek through the curtain.
And I see her. Evie.

She stands at Ghazt's side. We can faintly
hear her speaking into his shrivelly rat ear.

Sir, by my count, we have nearly five hundred zombie soldiers.

Is that, um, enough to begin our total terrible rule?

WE WILL WAIT AS LONG AS I SAY. I AM THE GENERAL.

Evie nods. "Of course, but the sooner we
release these zombies—the sooner they can DO
BAD!" she says, her voice cracking. "There are
human settlements to crush—and monsters to
enslave. We could start in Wakefield."

I gulp. Wakefield. Our home.

And human settlements. That could mean the people on the radio at the Statue of Liberty. That could mean every last survivor, everywhere.

Quick pause for a backtrack! For a long time, we thought we might be the only survivors of the apocalypse. But then, a few months ago, we found a radio and heard LIVE HUMAN VOICES and we were like, "Oh-Em-Gee-Whiz!"

There was a broadcast from an entire *colony* of humans hunkered down in the Big Apple! It was *major*. . . .

But then winter set in, and we couldn't go to NYC—and we haven't heard *anything* from the radio since. Quint and June are jazzed because there's a possibility their parents are still alive— but we can't leave Wakefield, because Evie and Ghazt are here doing bad stuff.

Still—Quint and June want to at least *know* if their parents might be OK. . . .

OK, un-pause the backtrack!

June leans in close. "If Ghazt ever stops being a complete lazy butt—we're all in trouble. Not just us—everyone . . . everywhere."

At that very moment, Dirk's claustrophobia goes from bad to ultra-bad. "I can't take that whispering, moaning sound anymore!" he says, grabbing his head, plugging his ears.

"Put a sock in it, dude!" June says.

Quint, being quite literal, removes his shoe, yanks off his sock, and stuffs it into Dirk's mouth. Toe jam flies. It's odd.

Dirk just about barfs up the sock. The next instant, he's tumbling through the curtain, bursting out from our hiding place.

"Dirk!" I cry, trying to stop him. "No!"

But it's too late.

Dirk's eyes are locked on a nearby claw-grab game—and the pair of headphones inside.

They're huge headphones, like hip DJs and air traffic controllers wear.

In a split second, our super-spy Mission Operation surveillance turns into what my old third-grade teacher would've called "a ruckus."

"I CAN'T TAKE THESE ZOMBIE MOANS!" Dirk cries out.

He grips the claw-grab machine. Then, with one mighty heave, brings it crashing to the ground.

SMASH!!! The Plexiglas case shatters—Dirk grabs the headphones and jams them onto his head.

The entire lair goes quiet. The old "could hear a pin drop" moment.

Then . . .

"Ahem." It's Evie.

Evie is staring at us.

Ghazt's staring at us, too.

And so is his army of the undead.

"Bring the dorky human ones before me," Ghazt says. His tail lifts and points at us, and then the zombies approach, arms raised, to drag us before their master.

chapter four

So now here we stand, in front of Ghazt and Evie. Captured prisoners! It kinda feels like we got caught texting in class and now we gotta face the principal. But we're not just staring down a few days of detention—our *dimension* is at stake!

Ghazt's massive form leans forward. His mouth opens, and I think he's about to eat us—but instead he just burps. Evie looks embarrassed. Ghazt readjusts, getting a grip on his whole belly-gas-burp situation.

"Argh—you!" he snarls, showering us with bits of cheesy spittle. "I should have taken my army and DESTROYED your little town when I had the chance."

I lean over to June and whisper, "Time for Mission Operation: Project Maximum Jack Confidence."

"Dude," June snarls. "If you say mission operation one more time—"

"So here's the deal, bad dudes," I say, taking a relaxed step forward, channeling my inner cool-guy Kurt Russell. "Right now, this entire joint is surrounded by monster warriors. So, either you release us—or I give the signal. And you don't want that, 'cause our monster buddies have itchy . . . um . . . itchy, uh . . . what's the—"

"Itchy backs?" Quint asks.

"No. Not itchy backs. Itchy, uh—itchy trigger fingers! That's it!"

"They mostly use swords and axes," June whispers. "Swords and axes don't have triggers."

"Fine! Itchy ax fingers! Whatever! Bottom line—Evie, Ghazt—release us, now, or I'm calling in the monster cavalry."

Wow, I really nailed that. That lie was so good that *I* almost believed it. Evie and Ghazt will never know it's a—

"BLUFF!" Evie shouts. "That's a bluff!" She leans toward Ghazt and whispers, "He's bluffing. Classic bluff. Kid's got bluff all over his face."

I scowl at Evie. She smiles in the most annoying way.

Ghazt's tail slithers up and tickles his lip in thought. "Hmm. Bluff. Bluffing. Bluffin. Muffin." Ghazt's stomach grumbles, then he says, "Evie, do we have any more of those little mini muffins I like? The blueberry ones?"

Evie clenches her jaw. Bites back a sigh. "No, sir."

I steal a quick glance to the side. Dirk's got his hands to his head, mashing the headphones hard against his skull.

No question—we need to make our move *now*. Evie and Ghazt don't seem to be on the same page. Maybe we can use that against them.

June picks up what I'm mentally throwing down—because she tilts her head and says, "Hey, Ghazt, if you're this *big, bad, zombie-controlling general*, how come Evie does all the talking while you just sit there on a big cheese throne?"

In response, Ghazt slurps cheese from a hollowed-out bowling ball.

WHAT'D THEY SAY? I FORGOT TO LISTEN, I WAS THINKING ABOUT CHEESE.

Sigh... She implied you were—ahem—lazy.

Ghazt doesn't like that. He snarls, then his tail snaps through the air. I hear a hollow thunderclap sound—the sound of Ghazt exercising his control over the zombies. . . .

Sure enough, the zombies begin to circle around us.

Evie approaches. "Jack," she says. "You are

unarmed. Bad move. I'm surprised you would show up without your precious blade. . . ."

I smile. "Y'know, Evie . . ."

That would have surprised me, too!

LEG BLADE! THAT'S RIGHT!

GASP

VELCRO RIP!

I whip the blade around, pointing it at Evie and Ghazt. Evie frowns. "You hid your Little League sword in your pants?"

"You bet I did," I say proudly.

"That's weird, kid."

"I'll tell you what's weird—*you*, ya weirdo, calling *me* weird! You're the weird one doing the weird worshipping! Now I hereby DEMAND you guys open a portal and LEAVE. Outta this dimension, post-haste! Whatever post-haste means. . . ."

Ghazt's tail snaps again—and the zombies inch even closer. June coughs into her hand, then says, very loudly, "WELL, JACK—IT APPEARS YOUR PLAN HAS FAILED."

"OK, geez, June—aggressive," I murmur.

June, again, louder: "I *SAID*, JACK, IT APPEARS YOUR PLAN HAS FAILED."

"Look, June," I whisper, "I know this is a big life-and-death moment—but you don't gotta be mean about it! It's not like—"

I SAID: WELL, JACK, IT APPEARS YOUR PLAN HAS FAILED!

And that's when I hear a sound like cannon fire erupting. The building shakes. The zombies stagger. Evie grabs Ghazt to steady herself.

I look up, just in time to see the ceiling practically evaporate as something like a meteor comes smashing through. . . .

chapter five

"June!" Quint happily exclaims. "You had backup waiting?!"

June grins. "Sure did."

I frown. "Was your backup plan code word 'JACK, IT APPEARS YOUR PLAN HAS FAILED?'"

June shrugs. "It worked, didn't it?"

"That is so messed up. But also I'm good with it 'cause it means I was *not* bluffing. YOU HEAR THAT, EVIE? I wasn't bluffing!"

Evie just glares and leaps back. A thin layer of water is trickling up through the floor. Biggun's meteor-like landing weakened the ground.

Ghazt descends from his disgusting throne. Bits of hardened cheese and melted chocolate stick to his fur. He snarls, "Seize them!" and his tail WHIP-CRACKS in the air. Instantly, the blue-robed zombies close in!

"Dudes," I say. "I'm going for the tail! You keep the zombies busy!"

"Happily!" Skaelka says.

Biggun just grunts and begins hurling zombies right and left. June and Quint are back-to-back, battling the Cabal of the Cosmic.

CRACK!

Ghazt's tail smacks me, and I'm hurled across the room. I land against a half-inflated pile of bowling lane bumpers.

Ghazt strides toward me, wading through his battling zombie horde. He darts forward and slashes his fat claw in my direction.

"Yikes!"

I dodge the attack by ungracefully flopping to the floor. His gnarled nails slice open big blue bumpers. There's a loud hiss, then an angry snarl as Ghazt claws his way through shredded rubber.

I *jab* the slicer, and Ghazt inches back. His whiskers twitch. His nose wrinkles. And a smile crosses his hideous face. . . .

"You know, Jack, during the horribly botched transference that brought me to your dimension, I adopted some of the rat's qualities. Including smell; and I smell the fear on you now, boy."

Just then, his beady eyes dart to the side—and his tail snaps. His powers seize a nearby zombie, and it's suddenly zipping across the room.

But not toward me.

Toward Quint.

The zombie's feet skim the ground and its outstretched arms thrash. Its broken jaw snaps menacingly. "Murrrr!"

"Quint!" I call out, but it's too late for any warning cries. The zombie is nearly upon my best buddy.

A horrifying bolt of cold fear explodes inside my brain: the image of Quint being bitten, being zombified.

I don't think.

I simply *act*.

I *swing* the Louisville Slicer toward the zombie, leaving a dark streak of energy in the air. And then—

I feel the Slicer *catch*—like the blade and
the zombie are connected by some strange
magnetism.

And all around, it's like someone hit the PAUSE
button on this battle. Everyone's looking at me.
My arms are unsteady and there's a zombie,
frozen, braced to pounce. . . .

I feel Ghazt's power tugging at the zombie, trying to push it toward Quint.

"No . . . you . . . DON'T!" I cry out, forcing the Slicer downward.

The hovering zombie is thrust down, too. Its knees buckle and it crumples to the floor in a drooling, groaning heap.

Jack. . . . How did you . . . ?

From the corner of my eye, I spot Skaelka sneaking up behind Ghazt. I need to keep him busy for one more moment.

Ghazt's icy rat eyes peer at me. Then the Slicer.

"Impressive," he laughs. "But it will not be enough to defeat me."

I shrug. "That's cool. I don't have to defeat you. I just have to distract you."

Ghazt grunts, "Uh?"

And Skaelka swings. . . .

Happy to finally use ax face!

Skaelka's razor-sharp blade slices through Ghazt's tail! The creature SHRIEKS. His eyes go wide and his face contorts into a "oh no now my tail is just a nub" face.

Instantly, every zombie STOPS. Their arms fall to their sides, stiff, like they're awaiting orders. They moan quietly. Drool falls.

Suddenly, water sloshes at our feet—it's old, grimy, and smells like someone forgot to flush. I realize Skaelka's ax must have split the floor, too.

Ghazt wobbles back and forth. Without his tail, he's off balance. He lurches to the side, then crashes heavily to the floor.

It cracks open even further.

I see a crisscrossing maze of pipes beneath the floor—and one massive sewer pipe, as wide as a train. The wood begins to crumble completely—like jigsaw puzzle pieces, falling away.

Ghazt's paws slap, his gnarled nails scrape the floor—but that only makes it worse. Water rushes up around him.

He lashes out, grabbing Evie.

Her eyes lock on to mine. She's stuck—and she knows it. She's scared. But more than that—I can tell she looks *mad*. She forces a never-admit-defeat smile. And then they are pulled under. . . .

And like that—Evie and Ghazt are swept up
in the rushing sewer water . . . gone.

"Whoa," I say. "Did we just beat the bad
dudes? Already?"

"We beat *these* bad dudes—yeah," June says.
"The threat is over—at least for a while."

I grin. "Rad. Mission Operation:
COMPLETE."

Quint approaches the severed tail. "Most important, we've removed Ghazt's ability to control zombies."

I glance around. Quint's right. The zombies don't move. They just stare at the tail. Eyes dull.

All of a sudden, Bardle comes sweeping into the room, stepping over the rubble.

IT SHOULD NOT BE UNEXPECTED. THE TAIL IS QUITE POWERFUL.

ALSO, THIS IS ME MAKING A DRAMATIC ENTRANCE.

Bardle doesn't seem to be enjoying this. He's not fist-bumping. He's not feeling the awesome.

"Bardle?" I ask. "Why aren't you feeling the awesome?"

"Yeah," June says. "We crushed that!"

"Exactly!" I say as I give Bardle a big ol' slap on the back. Which, I discover, is a bad idea, just awful, 'cause in a flash . . .

Whoa! Easy, dude!

SNIKT

A PALM TO THE BACK IS THE SIGN YOU WISH TO BATTLE TO THE DEATH.

IS THAT WHAT YOU DESIRE?

"Nope!" I say. "Totally not what I desire. In *this dimension*, a slap on the back just means, like, 'Hey, cool, good times, buddy—friendly back slaps!'"

Bardle's confused. "You slap for friendliness?"

"I mean—we don't say 'slap for friendliness' because that sounds deranged. It's just a—um—"

I'm trying to figure out how to explain when I realize—hoo boy—my hand *stings*.

It stings way worse than it should after a regular ol' friendly back slap. It feels like I jammed my hand into a flaming bonfire or grabbed a handful of red-hot coals.

"Argh,"I moan, shaking my hand back and forth. Thankfully, Rover bounds over and showers my palm with cold slobber. The pain subsides some. "Thanks pal, needed that."

Bardle grabs my wrist. Rover saliva splashes the ground as Bardle turns my hand over, examining it. He blinks quickly. "I suspect that using your blade to manipulate the undead causes it to become hot," he says. "So hot that wielding it becomes near impossible."

June stops walking. She cocks her head. Looks me up and down. Then she brings up the ninety-pound Dozer in the room. "Yeah . . ." she says slowly. "We should probably talk about the *craziness* that went down back there."

Quint's eyes are wide. "Jack," he says. "You *controlled* a zombie. . . ."

I kind of hoped no one would mention it, honestly. I feel a little numb. There's this feeling like *yay, that was rad*, but also kind of like *yah, this is scary*?

"I, uh. . . . I guess I did," I say with a weird little shrug.

Quint, Dirk, and June surround me. Like I'm a specimen at a laboratory. Like I'm some *new* Jack. Some *different* Jack.

Then, all together, they *explode*—

You got, like, **powers**, duder!

Kinda weird. Kinda rad.

You have the bootleg version of the Force!

"Wait, wait, hold up," I stammer. "I feel like there's a bunch of undeserved credit here. I didn't do anything! The Slicer did! And the Slicer just happens to be mine! I mean, it's just a Little League bat!"

Warmth creeps up my neck, across my cheeks.

"Aww, he's blushing!" Quint says.

June sees that I'm a big bit uncomfortable. Our eyes catch, then June winks at me. Super quickly, she says, "Yeah, but Jack will probably be lousy at the whole 'Slicer powers' thing anyway!"

Which is, like, a jab at me. But also a way of removing everyone's feeling that *wow, that was big*. The teasing—it makes it all feel normal again. And I appreciate the crud out of June for it.

"Look," I say. "I—uh—I felt the Slicer burn like that once before. With Ghazt, at the movie theater. But I didn't know it could do *that*. . . ."

My friends nod. Bardle's fingers trace his beard. It's quiet, and then—

Zombie moans. Loud.

"OK, enough raving about Jack's strange zombie-controlling ability. We must discuss *them*," Quint says, pointing behind us.

June sighs. "We cut off Ghazt's tail so that he couldn't control zombies anymore. But the zombies weren't supposed to *follow us*!"

Quint's hand shoots up like Hermione Granger in Potions class. "I will study the tail! I will uncover its secrets."

Bardle looks at Quint—like he's sizing him up. "Find a weakness in the tail," Bardle advises. "It may provide insight into weaknesses of *other* Cosmic Terrors."

Quint nods. "Wow. Using science to discover the vulnerabilities of interdimensional terrors. . . . I will *not* let you down!"

"But what do we *do* with these undead bozos?" I wonder aloud.

Skaelka pokes her head in with a scary solution to that problem. . . .

TWENTY-ONE MINUTES, THEN.

Bardle tugs at his rucksack as he thinks. "I suggest, strongly, that you keep them," he says. "Who knows what is to come . . . ?"

I shrug. "Fair enough. But where are we going to put four hundred zombies?"

"When my hamster died," Quint says, "my parents told me she went to live on a hamster farm."

"Your parents sound most deceptive!" Skaelka says happily. "A fine quality in a parental figure!"

June chuckles—she knows what Quint was getting at. "We can ask her," she says. "But she's not gonna be happy. . . ."

chapter seven

"She's not on the can . . ." June says, sighing and pushing through us. "Warg, it's June! We're here to give you—um—a really overdue thank-you."

Oh crud! I realize we never thanked Warg for the whole "saving our buddy from turning into a zombie" thing.

I mean, if your weird aunt sends you a bad book for Christmas—you have to write a *literal, physical* thank-you note! Warg gave us one of her EYEBALLS to save Dirk—yeah . . . that *definitely* deserves some gratitude. . . .

After a long moment, the door opens. It's not Warg—it's one of Warg's eyeballs, using its body to nudge open the door.

"You first," I whisper.

"No way," June says.

"I will go either *second or third*," Quint says. "Not first, not last."

"Aww, geez," Dirk groans, and he finally just shoves us all inside.

We're not greeted with a warm welcome.

I flash a grin. "Ahh, you're just saying that, Wargy. We're buds! And we owed you a major league thanks for saving Dirk!"

Warg glares. With every eyeball.

"Sooooo, we got you a thank-you gift!" I say.

"What is this gift?" Warg asks, brooding.

"Oh you're gonna love it! It's a—um—massive HORDE OF ZOMBIES! All yours! They're outside! Don't know where you wanna put them, but we thought maybe the Christmas tree farm? And that way they can't get out and bite us good folks and also you could maybe look after them? Again— this is a GIFT and you are SO, SO WELCOME."

"Jack's just rambling," Dirk interrupts.

"Am not!" I exclaim. "This is a wonderful gesture I'm doing. It's the gift that keeps on, uh, *decaying*!"

Dirk sighs. "Warg, I do wanna say thanks. They told me what you did. And I should, uh, return this."

Dirk reaches into his bag and pulls out—oh no. The eyeball. It's flattened and deflated—but it is most definitely the eyeball. . . .

I whisper, "Dude, you've been carrying that around this whole time?!"

"So cool . . ." Quint says.

The eyeball is gnarly. A month in a backpack can gnarly-fy *anything*. But a deflated eyeball? Massive nasty.

Warg silently takes it from Dirk and sets it on the ground. Dozens of eyeballs roll off her body, surrounding and inspecting the flattened one.

Thankfully, Bardle appears in the doorway, interrupting this slow-dance-level-awkward moment.

"Quint, June, Dirk—please, bring the zombies inside the farm's fence," Bardle says. "Jack stays."

Quint gives me a look, like I've been invited to do something special—and he hasn't. But then he flashes me a happy thumbs-up, because he's a bud like that.

Once everyone's gone, Bardle wastes no time. "Jack, tell Warg what happened. With your blade . . ."

"Uh, well," I say—and I realize I'm embarrassed and self-conscious. But I tell her everything.

When I've finished, all of Warg's eyes slowly inflate and deflate at the same time. I think it's the Warg version of, like, a deep sigh. Then she holds out her hand—palm open.

She wants the Slicer. I hesitate. I lost it once—and I won't let it happen again. But Bardle's neck gills flex and a rough-sounding grunt comes out.

I hand it over.

Warg runs her hand down the length of the Slicer. "Ghazt . . ." she says softly.

"Correct," Bardle says. "The power within that blade—it appeared when Ghazt's energy ripped into this dimension. . . ."

Just then, Warg's eyeballs return to her body. Dirk's deflated eyeball is gone. Eaten—absorbed, I guess—by the other eyeballs. They look almost restored now that they're back to their home base.

It's weird.

Warg rocks forward and says, "I do not want to see this world destroyed, like our home."

Bardle nods. "And that is why the power within this blade must become known."

Warg and Bardle exchange a long look. So long, in fact, that I say—

Warg looks at both Bardle and me. "You may keep the zombies here," she says reluctantly. Her mouth is a hard, stern line. "But—there is one condition."

"I don't have to watch you guys make out, do I?"

Bardle shoots me a look that says, "Don't embarrass me in front of the eyeball lady."

JACK SULLIVAN, YOU MUST LEARN THE LIMITS OF THIS WEAPON'S POWER. BARDLE WILL HELP.

"Wait, are you guys talking some training stuff?" I ask. "Am I about to get trained?"

Suddenly, the weirdness I felt about the zombies is gone because I am NUTSO PSYCHED that we're talking about training! I give Bardle a probably creepy smile.

Bardle shoots me a "who, me?" look, but I bet he's secretly fired up to be in on this, because whether he knows it or not, we're about to do a hardcore training montage. And literally ALL I HAVE EVER WANTED IS A HARDCORE TRAINING MONTAGE!

"YES!" I exclaim. "This is gonna be . . ."

Just then, June calls from outside. "Jack! Get out here! IT'S A PHOTO OP!"

Bardle and Warg follow me outside. My friends are hoisting Ghazt's tail onto the roof of an old hot cocoa stand.

"This is bigger than the biggest fish my ol' man ever caught," Dirk says, impressed.

I can see Dirk feels lousy. But he's fighting through it. Like when you have a birthday party or something, but then you get the flu but you DON'T WANT to miss it, so you force yourself to try to enjoy it even though you wanna collapse and maybe cry. Dirk's a trooper.

"Bardle, get in the pic!" June calls. "You too, Rover!"

We all gather close and smile our cheesiest smiles.

Just before Warg snaps the photo, I get this feeling. It's kinda like that feeling at the end of summer vacation when you see one of those stupid back-to-school sale signs, and it brings the whole perfect summer to a screeching halt; it hits you: these good times *end soon*.

Things are good now, but they might not be again for a long time. . . .

chapter eight

Two days pass. Two days of rest and recovery and then it's—

LEGENDARY HERO TRAINING! DAY ONE!

My alarm clock goes off—but I'm not even mad and I don't even hit snooze.

Y'know, funny thing about alarm clocks—you'd think during the Monster Apocalypse, you wouldn't need 'em anymore—'cause you'd just wake up every morning like . . .

What beasts shall I slay today? How many pints of goo shall I spill?

But nope.

Still love the snooze.

Except for today! Because today I TRAIN! The Slicer has powers and I must learn to wield those powers—and that is *totally* a Skywalker-style *call to adventure*!

The smell of breakfast carries me downstairs. If my nostrils aren't lying, it's Quint's famous donut hole kebab with chocolate syrup drizzle.

"Save some fancy donut sticks for me!" I shout as I toss on my hoodie and hop into the kitchen, trying to jam my feet into my sneakers without untying the laces.

I tumble into a chair and like an old-timey TV dad, I ask:

Soooo . . . what's everyone got in store for today?

"Well, dudes," I say. "All of your stuff sounds rad—and I wish I could drop everything and hang. But I've got hero training ahead of me!"

With that, Quint heads for Dandy-Lions ice cream shop across town—where he'll be studying the tail. June races upstairs to tinker with the radio. Dirk puts on his headphones, cranks up Metallica, and flops into our hammock. And I get my butt in gear.

I take an extra donut hole kebab for the road.
And one for Rover. And then two more in case
I get surprise hungry. And three more in case I
fall off Rover and sprain my ankle and I'm left,
starving, helpless, and in desperate need of
nourishment. And one more for good luck.

Outside, the air is crisp.

Rover's nostrils blow thick clouds of steam as
he charges across Wakefield toward the zombie
farm. My heart's pounding—I'm not sure if
I'm excited or if I'm anxious or if excited and
anxious are actually the exact same thing and
just no one told me.

When I get to the farm, Bardle is waiting
for me. The zombies are nearby, corralled in a
pen made from Christmas tree netting. I stride
toward Bardle, hand on my Slicer, and stop
when we're face-to-face. I'm patiently waiting
like a good little hero-in-training.

Bardle's face is stern. He's about to say some
intense mentor stuff, I know it. Here it comes—

"I smell donut holes," he says. "Have you been
eating donut holes?"

That was less intense than I expected.

"Oh, yeah, sorry. Should I not have eaten?
Is hero training like one of those doctor's
appointments where you can't eat before?"

"Did you bring me donut holes?"

"Um. Sure. . . ."

I toss him a fistful of donut holes (coincidently, *A Fistful of Donut Holes* is the title of my favorite Western). As he gulps them down, I'm feeling antsy—let's get this show on the road, right? This is it! This is . . . .

LEGENDARY HERO TRAINING. DAY ONE.

Wherein I, Jack Sullivan, begin the path to total zombie master manipulator!

SO, HOW DOES THIS WORK? WHERE DO WE BEGIN? WHAT DO I DO?

I frown. "Wait, huh—WHAT?"

"Where do we start?" Bardle asks.

"Why are you asking me? You're in charge of this thing! *You* tell *me* the game plan. Is it, like, punching bags of meat? Oh, I know! Moving rocks with my mind? Or maybe first—"

"I have no idea, Jack."

"Bardle—YOU are the trainer!" I exclaim. "The mentor! The mystical guide! Y'know—*do or do not* and all that junk."

Bardle scratches his nose fur, swallows another donut hole, and shrugs.

"Wait, so . . . you're *not* my mentor?" I'm about to kick the ground in frustration—when I realize . . . OF COURSE! This little roadblock is simply one of the challenges on my path to becoming a LEGENDARY HERO!

"OK, no worries, Bardle," I say. "I've watched enough movies with enough training montages to know exactly how this is gonna go down."

"Training montage movies?" Bardle asks, bewildered.

"YES!" I say. "See, first I'll be really lousy. But then there will be like seven minutes of training (I mean, it'll *actually* be days and days but it'll *feel* like seven minutes). But I'll *still* be lousy. Then I'll be like . . ."

The Seven-Eyed Shrieking Sea Beast!

Bardle looks unconvinced, but he doesn't have a choice. "We're DOING THIS," I say.

"Indeed, we are," Bardle says. "As soon as we finish the donut holes."

LEGENDARY HERO TRAINING. DAY TWO.

Wherein I, Jack Sullivan, freshly knowledgeable in the art of training, do some actual training! No donut hole distractions!

I need a target, like a bull's-eye, that I can try to get the zombies to attack.

So, I bring back the June Bait—the same weird dummy we used back when we were trying to catch a zombie. But I feel weird feeding June— even stuffed, dummy June—to the undead.

So, I mount the June Bait like a scarecrow, give it some new clothes, add a plastic Halloween ax, and pretty soon it's—

THE SKAELKA TARGET DUMMY!

I carefully approach the zombies, holding out the Slicer. . . .

I concentrate. Channeling my energy, going to my happy place; my inner Jack Sullivan happy sanctum. I *must* be able to command these dudes! And finally, after a long while . . .

Nothing happens!

Zip. Zero. Nada.

So I say, "OK, Bardle, never mind, I'm crummy at this. Let's do BMX bike jumps instead!"

We do.

So, days two, three, four, and five are pretty much as expected based on my hero training timeline. Lousy, next-level lousy, lousier, lousiest. Until . . .

LEGENDARY HERO TRAINING. DAY SIX.

Wherein I, Jack Sullivan, promise Bardle there will be no more BMX bike jumps and we will FINALLY DO RAD STUFF FOR REAL.

No messing around. Just pure focus. Inside my head, I repeat the words *Zombie, tackle the target! Zombie, tackle the target!*

Then I bring the Slicer whipping through the air and—

SPLAT

"The zombie moved! Bardle, did you see that? It moved!"

"I saw it fall over."

"Yeah and I'm the one that made it fall over!"

"Indeed," Bardle says wearily. "But it was not your intention to make it fall over."

"Y'know, you're a real glass-empty sorta monster, Bardle. Anyone ever tell you that?"

Then, suddenly—

I SHRIEK and drop the Slicer.

It's burning red-hot again—so hot I can't even hold it.

I pick it up anyway and sigh. Bardle's right—that was barely progress. And *more* progress will be difficult if each time I'm about to do something *legit*, the blade gets hot and my hand vibrates with that dark pain. . . .

But I keep trying.

And the blade keeps burning.

Finally, when the day is over, I groan, "Bardle, this is no good. I can't control one zombie—let alone a whole bunch of 'em! I mean, after nine hours—look at my lousy level of accomplishment!"

LEGENDARY HERO TRAINING. A BUNCH OF DAYS.

Wherein I, Jack Sullivan, definitely definitely succeed in my training! Even though I wanna give up!

Every day stinks. It's the same crummy day, on repeat: wake up early, try to do zombie-controlling coolness, fail.

On day thirteen, a botched Louisville Slicer move causes me to fall flat on my butt. That's when I finally say, "Bardle, I've *had it*! I'm going to play video games."

Bardle scowls. "You would give up so quickly?"

I shrug. I've faced so much: Blarg, Thrull, the King Wretch, Evie, Ghazt. . . . This shouldn't be hard! But it is.

It's a different kind of hard. This isn't something I can just slice or battle. This challenge needs something else, something new, something deeper. But I don't know what that is. . . .

I sigh and think back to the time *before* the Monster Apocalypse, only *nine months* ago:

Everything was simple then.

Everything is big now.

Nothing really mattered then.
Everything matters now.
This training is *important*.

And that's the thing—behind every swing of the Slicer, behind every attempt to *focus*—there's me knowing that, in a way, this power is the KEY to saving THE WORLD—and that the world depends on this; the world depends on ME.

That's a lot for one kid! I mean, how is ONE person supposed to protect everything and everyone?

It's unfair! It's LUDICROUS! The enormity of the task is too enormous!

"Bardle," I say. "I am playing video games. OK? That's the deal today. My choice."

Bardle takes a step, blocking my path.

There's something on his face I haven't seen before. His shoulders stiffen.

A sudden wind blows across the farm. A zombie toupee makes its escape.

The air around Bardle seems to still. His voice is heavy and gravelly as he says, "Jack, the time of Ṛeżżőcħ approaches. You must understand how important that is."

"I do . . ." I say. "But I also understand how important video game chill-out time is."

And then there is the cracking ROAR of Bardle's magic and—

Terror. Sudden terror. A pitch-black nightmare spreading wide, fully filling my vision. A monster bigger than the sky itself.

Fear rolls through me. I don't think. I just *do*. I swing the Louisville Slicer—a screaming strike that slashes into the darkness of the creature in front of me.

A creature that is not really there. . . .

The darkness disintegrates, and when the inky thing is gone I see—

A dozen zombies, on their backs.

I moved them.

I did that. I DID IT!

But then—PAIN! The blade—it becomes so hot that pain spreads to every molecule of my body. The Slicer falls to the ground. I collapse beside it, heaving, holding my burning hand.

"I'm sorry," I say with a heavy sigh. "Whatever this task is—I'm not up to it."

"That is not acceptable," Bardle says.

"But what if it's the truth? I mean—there are other survivors out there. And other not-evil monsters, like you. What are *they* doing? Why is all this MY JOB?"

And I laugh, because it reminds me of when your teacher assigns a group project but picks partners for you and you end up doing everything. That's what this is like, only this group project is SAVE THE ENTIRE DIMENSION FROM AN UNTIMELY END!

". . . End," I say, thinking aloud now. And then, quietly, "Bardle, could I ask you a question? A serious one?"

Bardle nods.

"When this all ends—*if* this all ends—do you want to, like, go home?"

Bardle simply says, "My home is destroyed. It is Ṛeżżőch's now."

I look up at him, squinting. The afternoon sun bounces off the hilt of Bardle's sword and showers us in orange light. "Then what do you, like, want?" I ask. "I mean, everyone has to *want* something. I learned that in English class."

Bardle waits a long while before he answers.

WHEN ALL IS SAID AND DONE, I WANT TO HAVE BEEN USEFUL. TO HAVE MATTERED.

I think that's a pretty good answer. I'd like the same thing. To matter is—

Suddenly, I hear the rumble of an engine.

I leap up and see Big Mama speeding across the horizon, Quint at the wheel! What the huh? No. *What the DOUBLE HUH?* June's in the back!

They're off adventuring! Without me!

One of the lousy parts of this training thing—apart from *being* lousy at this training thing—is that it's taking me away from my buds!

Like, last week, I went back to the tree house—and Quint, June, and Dirk were laughing and sharing an inside joke. That's right—an inside joke that I WAS NOT A PART OF. *LITERALLY MY WORST NIGHTMARE.*

Jack will never get this!

Had to be here!

I am so happy it's only us making this joke together!

Even I think it's funny!

OK, it wasn't exactly like that—but you get the idea. Anyway, I think, *Nope, right now, I will not let my friends create new inside jokes unless I am inside those inside jokes, helping to create them, from the inside.* . . .

I race away from the farm, shouting over my shoulder, "Bardle, gotta see my friends it's urgent friendship business be back!"

I've got a brutal cramp in my side and my goofy light-up sneakers are going haywire when I finally catch up to Big Mama.

Huffing, puffing, I see—

There's a big metal contraption hanging off the side of the truck! What are they doing—fishing for air monsters?!

Then Quint and June spot me and give me a look like, "Wut."

I collapse against Big Mama and manage to say, "I have caught you guys and your . . . inside joke . . . *gasp* . . . building . . . *gasp* . . . operation . . . *gasp*."

But that's when I see it, in the back.

The radio.

Oh.

We've heard *zero* out of the radio since that last broadcast, months ago, at Fun Land.

I sigh. This inside joke is *not* funny.

Quint and June are looking at me like I might break. Like I'm a super tall tower of Legos that might topple over at any moment. I guess I made quite an impression back when . . . y'know . . . I had my **MAJOR MELTDOWN**.

"Hey," I say, snapping out of it. "I hope you can make it work. For real."

Quint smiles warmly and sticks his hand out. I grab his wrist, and he pulls me up into Big Mama.

There's something solemn and heavy in the air—like we're all thinking about *big things*.

I look down at the blade—and at my hand.

"How goes the training, young Jedi?" Quint asks.

"Dude, honestly, it STINKS and I'm THE STINKIN' WORST. I thought it was gonna be like *The Karate Kid*. Or *Rocky*. But it's more like—I dunno—a movie about a dude who never succeeds ever."

I sigh. I want to just go home with my buds and flop on the couch and watch movies and eat food and flick dry boogers out the window.

And I decide—I need a break from training. Desperately. Because I'm getting way frustrated—so frustrated I might just give up forever.

And I can't do that, because the Slicer and its weird power—they're gonna help keep us alive. All of us: Quint, June, Dirk . . .

"Wait a sec," I say. "Dirk's not here. Where's the big guy?"

June frowns. "Same place he's been all week—lying around, headphones on, music blasting. We tried to get him to come, but he shrugged us off."

I look at June. "Then I know what we gotta do. Quint might be busy studying the tail, but our buddy Dirk is down in despair. And an in-despair buddy demands drastic measures. A mission *operation* even. That's right, I'm talking . . ."

I look up at proud, posing June. "That's all fine and well, but usually I'm the one who announces the big plans and junk."

"Deal with it, Sullivan," she says with a sly smile. And that smile makes me smile.

chapter nine

"Right, sorry," June says quickly. "I got excited."
Dirk groans and flips over onto his side.
"Dudes, I don't need cheering up."

"You're *sleeping* on a trampoline," June says.

"You cannot be bummed out on a trampoline," I say. "Physically impossible."

June shrugs. "Yet here he is. Bummed out. On a trampoline."

"Dudes, be quiet and leave me alone," Dirk grumbles. "I got these big headphones on 'cause I don't want to hear the outside world. Get me?"

I nod. "I get you, but TOO BAD, YOU'RE COMING WITH US! June and I planned a whole day of cheering-up activities. You will never know happiness, Dirk, like the happiness you will know THIS DAY! June, what is the *first* cheer-up activity?"

June looks at our list—and frowns. "Have fun on the trampoline."

"Oh. Crud. Well . . . Crud."

We're off to a lousy start. And it only gets lousier. . . .

We try everything: bad-movie marathon, chili cook-off, garlic knot juggling, loogie-spitting contest, and even a mosh pit dance party.

After our nineteenth failed cheer-up-Dirk attempt, June says, "Y'know—maybe it's not cheering up Dirk needs. Maybe he's just gotta, like, *relax*."

"Ooh, like a massage?" I suggest. "That's what people on TV do when they need to relax."

So, we drag Dirk to the spa where all the moms and dads used to go before Valentine's Day to get last-minute gift certificates, and, well . . .

THIS IS NOT RELAXING!

Another failure. A massage meltdown.

"June," I say. "If we're gonna do this, we need to go to the place where I do my *best* thinking!"

"Not following you to the toilet," she says.

"Not the toilet," I say as I walk toward Big Mama. "I do my best reading on the toilet. But my best *thinking* requires an entirely different atmosphere. . . ."

See, I do my best brain-work when I'm playing video games. I know that just sounds like an excuse to play video games, but seriously—it's like gaming clears your head enough that you can really *think*, but you still zone out enough that you don't *overthink*.

And it's even better when it's . . .

FOOTBALL FIELD VIDEO GAMES!

Quint had the brilliant idea to hook up our consoles to the jumbo screen at the high school's football stadium.

Right now, June and I are playing *NIMBUS: Battle Royale* while Dirk snoozes in Big Mama's backseat. The windows rattle from his seismic snoring.

I've just finished blasting June with a sniper crossbow when June sets down the controller. "I hope your thinking is working," she says, "'cause we need to do *something*. Dirk is sadder than—than—"

I complete her sentence. "Sadder than end-of-the-world online video games."

"End-of-the-world online games are monster-truck-sized *miserable*," June says. "Remember when this game was a super intense, fight-to-the-death battle royale against people from all over the world? Everyone for themselves—last man standing wins?"

I nod. "Before the world ended—it was constant online combat!"

But now . . . it's just a digital dust bowl. A wasteland. When June and Quint and I first sat down to play, it felt like the *game* world had entered apocalypse mode, too. . . .

But Quint used his genius brain to hook up multiple consoles, so at the very least, the three of *us* could play each other.

But alas, this gaming session is not giving me any brilliant make-Dirk-happy ideas.

Just then, I hear an engine bark: a BoomKart, roaring across the football field. I glance back and see Quint sliding to a stop, wheels kicking up turf. "Ooh, playing *NIMBUS*?" Quint shouts as he hops out. "Toss me a controller, friend!"

Quint climbs up into Big Mama and plops down on the couch beside us. He's covered in rat hair and tail guts. And he's got Dirk's old-timey football helmet on his head, with wires and knobs jutting out every which way.

"Cool hat," I say—and at first I mean it sarcastically, but it actually *is* a pretty rad hat-helmet.

"It's designed to help my brain waves pick up the energy emitted by the tail," Quint explains. "But no luck yet. It's not easy doing it alone. Bardle checks in sometimes, but it's like he doesn't even *want* to learn its secrets."

I'm trying to pay attention to Quint, but my eyes pan down to his disgusting, Ghazt-goo-glazed thumbs on the joysticks. I almost barf. You know how annoying it is when a buddy gets Cheeto powder or Dorito dust on your good controller? This is the same thing, but nineteen times worse—it's interdimensional rat-tail innards!

Quint clicks into the game—and a notification pops up on screen: NEW PLAYER HAS ENTERED.

All of a sudden, June's eyes bug out and she leaps to her feet.

"GUYS!" she says. "Listen, listen, listen! Maybe the radio has been silent because the survivors found a *better* way to communicate? Maybe they went *online*! Using games like a big message board!"

We could find out about our parents!

Plus, all the work we put into the radio—it isn't wasted! We can hook it up the same way, but instead of trying to pick up radio signals . . .

We try to pick up Wi-Fi using our video game systems.

Whoa!

If June's right . . . this is MAJOR! It means we could play *Battle Royale* the real way! With other humans! And—

Oh. Right. June's talking about finding her family. That's more important.

But her stroke of genius gives me an idea. Just then, I glance back at Dirk in the backseat.

I yank the couch-a-pault lever, hurling myself to the turf, then dash around the side of Big Mama.

Dirk is sprawled out in the back, snoozing, feet out the window. I grab his sneakers and bang 'em together. "DIRK! When we created our own traditions for the holidays, do you remember what yours was?"

Dirk's groggy. "Dude, I'm napping."

"You *hate* napping."

"Well, I like it now," he grumbles. "When your head is a bad place to be—it's nice to turn it off for a bit."

That's too deep for me right now, so I just remind him, "You were all about KING OF THE HILL. . . ."

I AM OVERCOME WITH JOY!

BOOSH

"Buddy, listen," I say. "No one ever needed cheering up more than you do right now. You love King of the Hill, and *Battle Royale* is video game King of the Hill, so—"

Dirk grunts and rolls over, facedown. June and Quint are excitedly discussing the Wi-Fi. They're like two parrots, trying to out-yap each other.

But me? I feel a plan forming. A plan to fix my buddy. I'm thinking, noodling, ideas swirling, and finally I scramble up onto Big Mama and I just explode—

chapter ten

Back in town, I can't contain my excitement! We're throwing a *real-life* Battle Royale *right here in Wakefield*!

Skaelka yells, "YES! Combat! Finally!"

Before I can explain the rules, there's a CLANG. And then another. The sound of real weapons. At the first mention of battle, the monsters are unsheathing interdimensional swords and brushing off monstrous maces!

"WAIT! WAIT! HOLD UP!" I shout. "False alarm. Misunderstanding! Last Creatures Standing is a *game*!"

Skaelka's confused. "You mean—no actual death battling?"

"Um. No. No death battling," I say.

"A little bit?" Skaelka asks.

"Nope."

"One or two bits?"

"Zero bits, Skaelka. Zero bits."

Skaelka grumbles. Monsters gripe.

Thankfully, June saves the day. "The reason it's not a *real* battle," June says, "is because that would be *too easy for you*! This way—it'll be a challenge. A Big Gulp, behemoth-sized challenge."

Skaelka's eyes go wide. "Skaelka likes a challenge. Not as much as Skaelka likes death battling, but Skaelka will take what Skaelka can get."

But some monsters aren't convinced. See, ever since the Monster-Human Olympics, our creature buddies have been crazy competitive. It's not enough to win—they need *proof*.

"What prize does the victor receive?" one monster shouts.

"Is it the large intestine of a kromlin, to be worn like a necklace?" one calls out.

"Or is it the small intestine of a kromlin, to be worn like a bracelet?" another asks.

We're staring out at a sea of skeptical monster faces. Skaelka runs a finger along her ax and says, "What is this *Tremors II* that you speak of?"

Quint looks at me, shrugs, and I decide to commit to the lie. "Oh," I say. "On Earth, *Tremors II* is like, um, *the ultimate prize*. Yeah. Only the most courageous warriors are honored with *Tremors II*. If you have a copy of *Tremors II*, you're basically THE ULTIMATE."

The monsters huddle up. There's a lot of whispered discussion.

And then—

chapter eleven

Three days later, it's nearly *Battle Royale*. But A LOT happened in three days. A quick list:

- Dirk sulks and sleeps—nothing else. Something's seriously wrong.

- I train a bunch—and I fail a bunch. My life is not the epic training montage I had in mind. . . .

- Quint studies the tail—and gets tail guts everywhere. There's now a semi-permanent layer of goo on the toilet seat, and let's just say, that toilet has seen enough.

- June locks herself in her room, fully focused on figuring out how to turn video game Wi-Fi into a "find the humans" apparatus.

- Also, Rover is cute. Super cute. As usual.

And then, at last, it is REAL-LIFE *Battle Royale* time. . . .

The Town Square is kinda like the game's lobby—we're all gathered around, decked out in full Last Creatures Standing gear. And by gear, I mean . . . weird junk. We have gone MAXIMUM LEVEL in the costumes and skins department.

We're posing with radical gear so
we look cool. During the game,
all tools and weapons will be hidden
in LOOT CRATES!

We'll be battling in Duo Mode—teams of two players, facing off against one another, and the last team standing wins! I suggested duos so that I could partner up with Dirk. . . .

'Cause that's the *real* point of this game: finding out what's bothering my buddy.

When your friend is hurting, that's serious biz. And if it's gonna take the fog of war for me to pick his brain, so be it. . . .

"PLAYERS, LISTEN UP!" Quint shouts as he leaps into the rules. I sort of zone out, because it's all standard battle royale stuff. But there are two big exceptions:

#1: LOOT CRATES: *Quint-made weapons, like football launchers, NERF cannons, etc., have been hidden in LOOT CRATES across town. Vehicles, too! Find them and use them against your foes!*

In a video game, the loot crates just sort of spawn randomly. Sadly, we don't have random loot crate spawn powers—so we got Biggun to place loot crates and vehicles all over town.

And the #2 big important difference: *GOO-SLIME.*

Just like a video game, when a player is out, they're out—no faking! But we needed a way to make sure no one cheated. I mean, we've all played flashlight tag with that one kid who totally gets caught but is still somersaulting around like, "Nope, you missed me! Nope, you didn't see me!"

That kid is the worst.

Don't be that kid.

Thankfully, Quint came up with gleaming, glowing goo-slime! When he first explained it to the monsters, he sounded like a late night infomercial host. . . .

Goo-slime! Every weapon is loaded with it! If you get hit, the substance will slow you down and stop you in your tracks. So, you're effectively out!

Quint put Skaelka in charge of goo-slime
weapon assembly. So, for the past three days,
the monsters were holed up inside Joe's, doing a
Santa's workshop thing.

I can only imagine how *that* went. . . .

I NEED THREE
HUNDRED GOO-
SLIME WEAPONS—AND
I NEEDED THEM
YESTERDAY!

I glance over at Dirk—I see he's struggling.
He's sort of staring off into space, not blinking.
I can't wait any longer to make him better, so I
elbow Quint. "Time to get the show on the road."

Quint lifts his multipurpose remote above his head and bellows over the crowd, a feverish grin crossing his face as he flicks a toggle and—

Fireworks rocket off the roof of the tree house and zoom into the air! The world's first—and only—real-life game of *Battle Royale* has begun. . . .

chapter twelve

We're not even five minutes into this thing, but I feel like I've already won because this is SO gonna cheer up Dirk.

But also, we're gonna win for real, in a legit victory way! See, we have an advantage: *my encyclopedic knowledge of video games!* I know the best way to win a *Battle Royale* melee is to:

1. Find a vehicle.
2. Cruise around in that vehicle, avoiding other players, until you find a loot crate.
3. Take your loot crate gear and hide out in a safe location while the other players battle it out! When there's nearly no one left, you simply—
4. SWOOP IN FOR ULTIMATE VICTORY!

I'm trying to explain that to Dirk when suddenly, zipping past the mouth of the alley ahead of us is Skaelka. And *what the huh*—she already completed Step 1. I crane my neck, looking up at her ridonculous monster vehicle.

She's inside the rusted husk of a 1980s Snatcher convertible. But that car frame is, in fact, the shell of a sort of other-dimensional hermit crab. It is—

-The Carapace-

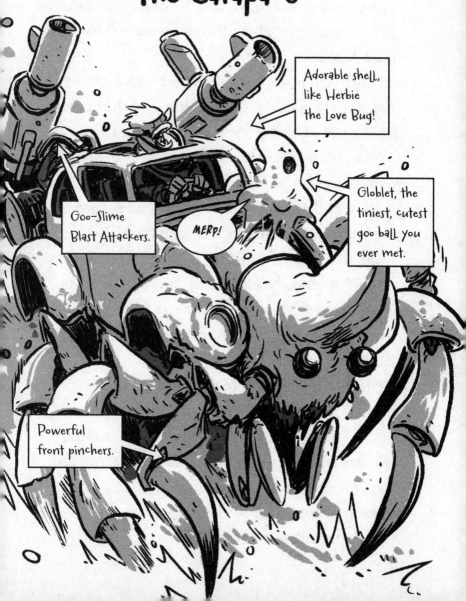

Skaelka's partnered with Globlet, a creature that resembles a tiny, very huggable wad of gum. Skaelka and Globlet must have already found a loot crate, because they've got two massive Goo-Slime weapons pointed at us.

"Hello, human Sullivan," Skaelka says with a grin. I'm staring down the barrel of a Goo-Slime Blast Attacker.

I gulp. Oh man, we *cannot* get knocked out of the game this early—I haven't had a chance to get heart-to-heart honest with Dirk yet.

Thankfully, at that very second, *two more monsters* come screaming down the street. They're riding souped-up, motorized scooters—and they unload on Skaelka and Globlet.

Skaelka ducks. Globlet dodges. The slime assault misses. "Jack, you are lucky this time," Skaelka says. Then she turns the Carapace around, charging toward her enemies.

Phew.

OK. Vehicle time. We need our own.

And I need answers from my buddy.

"So, Dirk . . ." I say as we duck-and-run our way across Wakefield. "You've been acting all sorts of sad and weird. You wanna, like, talk about it? Chit-chat?"

Dirk doesn't even respond.

"See, if you're feeling down," I continue, "sometimes it helps to talk to buds about your feelings—"

"STOP!" Dirk roars, snapping. "Dude, I'm trying to play this real-life video game. Remember—*your idea*. And if you'd pay attention, you'd hear what I hear."

I pause and listen. "The sounds of romance?"

"No, dude. A BoomKart engine."

I listen harder. He's right! I spot it: across the street, inside the SunOil gas station, is an idling BoomKart.

"PERFECT! Finding a vehicle is Step 1 in winning a battle royale. C'mon!"

The gas station's window is long gone. I try to do an action hero hop through, but I fall and land on my nose. Dirk simply struts through the front door like a normal human. He glares at me.

Crud. Don't need grumpy Dirk glares.

The whole point of *Battle Royale* is for Dirk to have some fun. And if he's staring daggers at me—then he's having *less than fun*.

"Look, bro," he says, pointing. "Found one of your lame treasure chests."

"Not a treasure chest," I say. "LOOT. CRATE."

While I hop into the BoomKart, Dirk opens the crate. He finds something sweet.

"Mallet now, feelings later," Dirk grunts as he climbs onto the back of the BoomKart.

"Hang on tight!" I say, hitting the gas, bursting through the door, and speeding outside. "Now we just avoid everyone else while they take each other out. Then: VICTORY!"

KA-SCHLOOM! GOO-BOOM!

Spoke too soon.

Goo-Grenades are raining down upon us.

Wez and Fern, two flying monsters from Joe's,

are swooping in. Wez is armed with a Goo-Crossbow—and it's aimed directly at Dirk.

"Not today!" Dirk barks as he reaches up and *grabs* Wez's leg. Which is maybe bad, because Dirk's strong, and now we're airborne. . . .

Wez and Fern whip us through the sky. We get a nice aerial view of the game, and I'm just seeing the skate park come into view when suddenly, a high-pitched whistling fills the air.

"Incoming!" Dirk cries out.

I glance down—and see a stream of goo-slime rocketing upward, streaking toward us. It's another monster team, but I can't make out who it is. Wez veers right and *DROPS* the BoomKart. We're suddenly falling through the air!

"JACK, I HATE THIS GAME!" Dirk shouts as we plummet.

"NO YOU DON'T YOU LOVE IT AND IT'S MAKING YOU FEEL SO MUCH BETTER!" I shout, and then—

CLANG! The BoomKart lands atop the roof of Wunder Wiener, the local hot dog joint. I scramble out while Dirk readies his Goo-Mallet. Dirk's squinting, even though there's no sun. Dirk's cool like that.

Wez and Fern swing back around, diving through the air like synchronized swimmers. They zoom toward us, Dirk swings his mallet, and—

SMACK!

Goo-slime explodes! With one blow, Dirk takes them both out! Wez and Fern drop their weapons and are sent arcing upward, tumbling, sailing, end over end. Their wings beat the air as they perform a slow, spinning spiral descent.

"Revenge will be ours, humans! But it will be friendly revenge because we realize it is only a game!" Fern cries out as she disappears over the tree line.

A moment later, our walkies hiss: "Wez and Fern here, sadly reporting that we are out of the game. Defeated by Team Dirk and Jack. . . ."

I happily scoop up Wez's Goo-Crossbow. Glancing around, I'm like—ROCK ON! We're at Wunder Wiener, at the edge of the skate park. We've got an elevated position—PERFECTO!

"So, let's hang tight for now," Dirk says.

I nod and point toward the park entrance. "Stay low—creatures incoming."

A dozen monsters descend on the park in pure chaos. We're like those lucky dudes who get to watch the World Series from the roof of their apartment or whatever—we have a full bird's-eye view of the action.

And the action is white-knuckle intense. . . . Full-blown battle-o-rama.

Players are defeated. Loot is dropped. Gear is scooped up. And then, like any *Battle Royale* game, the action moves on. Players shift to a new location to battle over a new loot crate.

Now. This is my moment.

No more delaying—I gotta find out what's wrong with Dirk. As we wriggle on our bellies toward the edge of the Wunder Wiener roof, it feels like we're tough-as-nails space marines in some tough-as-nails space marine war movie. And what do tough-as-nails space marines talk about while they survey a galactic battlefield? FEELINGS!

"So, Dirk . . ." I say.

I can practically feel him groan. "If I tell you, will you shut up?"

"Honestly? No, probably not. I could try! But my mouth kinda just goes and goes. . . ."

Dirk grumbles. Then—

OK, here's the deal. I'm hearing stuff.

Stuff that's not there. Sometimes it sounds like static. And sometimes like voices . . .

Oh. Um . . . Wow.

Before I can think of something helpful to say, Dirk ends the conversation. "Don't wanna talk about my brain anymore."

I nod. "Fair enough."

"But," he says, "I will admit—this Last Creatures Standing thing is kinda dope."

I smile. I got him to open up a little *and* he's having fun! Mission Operation: Cheer Up Dirk— *kinda* being accomplished!

"And it's about to get even more dope," he says. "Look! Another loot crate!"

I see the crate—it's hidden beneath a ramp down in the skate park pool: the Pit. It's sitting there like a big, fat, killer Christmas present just waiting to be opened.

"Dirk, that's no ordinary loot crate. That's the massive, hard-to-find loot crate every game has."

"Let's get it," Dirk says, and even though that goes against all my winning tactics—I'm just happy to see Dirk excited. So, I follow him, scrambling down from Wunder Wiener, then racing across the park, heads up, alert, eyes open for possible enemies.

We're nearly there, down into the Pit, when the ground starts to shake.

chapter thirteen

"It feels like an earthquake!" I cry out.

"Like a monstrous earthquake," Dirk adds.

I'm sliding down one of the half-pipe ramps, trying to surf the slick concrete curve, when the ground shakes again. I lose my balance. Dirk tumbles after me and we both land in the Pit.

We recover, rising, shaking off bits of gravel.

I gulp. "What the . . ."

The earth trembles again, and I stumble back into Dirk's arms. It's a cozy hold, I'm not ashamed to say. I bet my dude gives good snuggles.

Something is rolling and bouncing toward us. Stepping back, I see it over the lip of the sloping wall.

At first, I think it's some cartoonish, giant-sized tumbleweed. Then it comes into focus—and I gasp. It is—

This wild eyeball almost turned me and Quint into human pincushions at the graveyard last year!

The Hairy Eyeball Monster

The creature careens through the fence, slamming through a rail and plunging into the park's flat-bottomed pit.

As the eyeball rolls—zigzagging like a short-circuiting robot gone berserk—I can tell it's different. The Hairy Eyeball Monster is now COVERED IN VINE-THINGIES!

"It's like a mammoth meatball rolled around in monster spaghetti!" I cry.

The monster's shriek is not one of those I'm-evil-and-I'm-angry-'cause-you're-botching-my-plans shrieks that someone like Evie would make. No—this is a shrill moan of suffering.

"I think it's scared," I say. "I think it's hurting!"

Dirk nods. "The vines. They're, like, choking it or something!"

The eyeball frantically rolls back and forth. It looks so helpless, wrapped in green strands, like a game of tetherball gone wrong.

Suddenly, not thinking, I bark into the walkie, "Guys, new rules! Whoever frees the Hairy Eyeball Monster will be named Last Creatures Standing!"

Silence over the walkie. And then Skaelka: "You mean—we free the beast and we receive the *Tremors II* VHS?"

"Yes, sure, fine!" I shout as I dive to the side, just barely avoiding the rolling ball of terror. "*Tremors II* for everyone!"

Chaotic static erupts on the walkie channel. It sounds like every monster in town stops mid-battle to head in our direction.

"On your feet, bud!" Dirk barks as he yanks me up. The eyeball lurches at us. We brace for impact, but there's a deafening—

CRACK!

The eyeball snaps back.

"The vines have snagged on the half-pipe!" Dirk shouts. "It's like a dog on a leash—it can only go so far."

"Dirk, I got an idea!" I shout. "Remember in school, when we had to run laps? Follow me!"

We start sprinting circles around the perimeter of the half-pipe and the Hairy Eyeball Monster follows. With each loop, the creature is twisted more and more tightly in the vines. Soon, it's pinned to the wall—the vines wrapped around it holding it still.

"Now!" I say to Dirk. "Let's destroy the vines."

Dirk smiles. "MALLET MELEE!!!"

Each goo-slime-covered swing melts, slices, and tears through the vines! Soon, only one titanically thick Vine-Thingy still chokes it.

Dirk raises his hammer—but the vine tangles around it. He tries to wrestle it away, but it's tugged from his hands. The force hurls him across the Pit, into a metal railing.

It's up to me now. I'm jamming a goo-slime can into the crossbow when—

The vine lashes out at me! I aim the bow, but before I fire—

SNAP!!

The vine breaks free from the wall and the Hairy Eyeball Monster barrels after me. I turn to run—but there's no place to run *to*.

I'm trapped.

The Pit's steep, curved side is like a wall. I slide and fall repeatedly. This is built for skateboarding and biking—I'd need to be an *American Ninja Warrior* dude to climb out!

The Hairy Eyeball Monster rocks back and forth. A misty sheen glistens over its body—I'm not sure if it's stress-sweat or tears or both.

It begins rolling toward me, the one huge vine both propelling and choking it. The Hairy Eyeball Monster is nearly done for.

And I'm nearly done for, too.
Then, Skaelka and June come out of
nowhere—

Behind Skaelka's Carapace is an army of Joe's Pizza monsters, at the ready.

Yes! MULTIPLE PLAYERS HAVE ENTERED THE GAME!

"Your puny game weapons will not conquer these vines!" Skaelka says. "I must chop!"

"I think our puny weapons might actually be perfect!" June smirks as she slams a goo-slime cartridge into the Gift and unloads!

June's goo-slime pounds the Vine-Thingy that encircles the Hairy Eyeball Monster. It sizzles and crackles—then hardens on the vines.

I call to the monsters: "MISSION OPERATION: FREE THE HAIRY EYEBALL! FIRE AT WILL!"

And they do. . . .

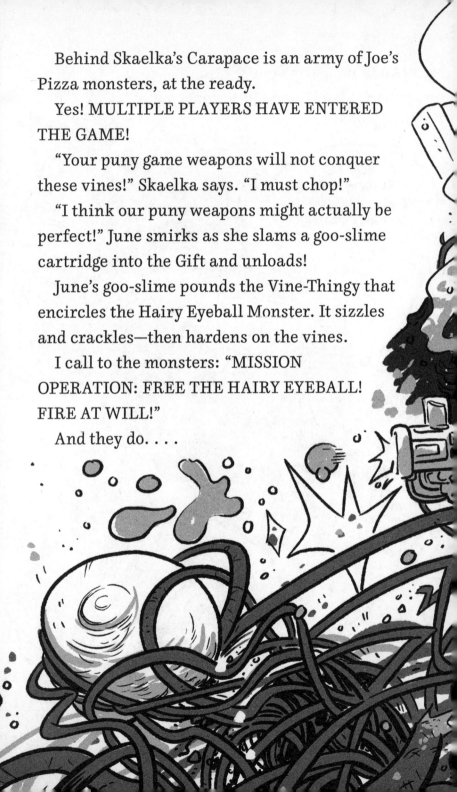

When the smoke clears, the eyeball shivers on the cracked pavement. Its body is translucent. The Vine-Thingies turn to ash. Our monster buddies all take a solemn step back.

I'm not sure what to do—I just know the creature doesn't deserve to hurt like this.

Suddenly, there is a massive thundering sound. "Quint, get back!" I shout.

Vine-Thingies burst through the pavement, like hundreds of spindly branches. They clutch the Hairy Eyeball Monster!

GRABBED!

The monster shrieks and struggles, but it's no use. An instant later, the eyeball is *gone*—pulled, howling, into the crumbling pavement. . . .

And then the vines snake toward us! They're like tentacles—horrible, hungry, insatiable tentacles! And they want me and all my buddies!

"Look! More vines!" Quint starts to say, pointing inside the gaping hole.

But I just grab him and shout, "NOT NOW!"

Skaelka's Carapace zooms by—and I quickly grab the car-shell's rusted bumper. It pulls us up, out of the skate park bed.

When we've reached a safe distance, we catch our breath. We watch the Vine-Thingies slither and search—then, together, slip back into the ground with a horrifying—

HOOOOOOWWWWWWLLLLL!!!!

Quint's still huffing and puffing. "If the Vine-Thingies pulled one monster into the ground," he says, "they could pull more."

"They nearly did," I say.

June's face is tight with concern. "This threat is new, unexpected—and clearly growing," she says. "Growing, it seems, right beneath our feet."

A moment later, June's concern turns to flat-out panic. Her eyes dart around. "Where's Dirk?"

I feel my stomach drop. "He was with us, just a moment ago, but—"

"There!" Quint says. "Oh no. He's going toward that horde of zombies!"

One of Quint's Zom-B-Gone torches burns near the edge of the park, and Dirk lumbers toward it like some sort of sleepwalking shadow. . . .

By the time we catch up to him, he's past the torch. A fence cuts him off and he stands perfectly still, gazing down at the road below.

There are zombies down there.

They stare up at Dirk. And he stares back at them.

Dirk's eyes are foggy and his expression is stiff. It reminds me of something. . . .

Finally, June manages to pull Dirk away— snapping him out of his stupor.

I put my face close to his and wave my hand. "Hey, buddy. Where you been?"

He swats me away. "Uh, here?" he says, confused. Then he stomps away.

Quint, June, and I exchange nervous looks. MISSION OPERATION: CHEER UP DIRK wasn't just a failure—it was worse than that. Way worse. . . .

chapter fourteen

Later, back at the tree house, Dirk settles into his usual gloomy state—headphones on, music blaring, eyes shut.

I want to fix Dirk. I want to help him. But I don't know how. Something's wrong with him—and he's getting worse, not better.

I'm thinking of striking up another convo to get more out of Dirk, when I hear giggling upstairs.

It's Quint and June—they're up there, laughing about something! What could be more important than our buddy's well-being? Some hot new inside joke . . . ?

Moments later, I'm banging on June's door.

I glance at the TV. On it is a scrolling list of names. Bertie Farn. Henry Fenklemeier. Suzie Fenklemeier.

"It's names," I say, confused. "It kinda looks like a—"

"A snow day!" June says. "Or a storm day! How they list all the schools that have the day off—y'know? And now—look. . . ."

Quint says, "The Statue of Liberty broadcast—it's not on the radio anymore, but it's *here*. It's a list of names. Repeating. Each name is a person who has checked in as 'SAFE' during the Monster Apocalypse."

This is big.

Bigger than big. So big that, for a moment, I also forget about Dirk.

Softly, I say: "It's on the letter F."

Quint nods. "It's slow. By my calculations, it'll be weeks until it comes back around to the beginning of the alphabet. To B—for Baker. And D—for Del Toro. But, Jack—it works! June's idea worked!"

"We're going to record it," June says. "So there's no chance we miss any names."

I turn and leave.

From the hall, I hear June leaping to her feet. "Jack, don't freak out," she says. "We just want to find our families. Don't be mad!"

I poke my head back in the room and grin. "I'm not mad. I'm getting popcorn! Can we make fun of people's weird names together?"

June looks at me. "Yes," she says. "Yes, we can."

"Good. Be right back!"

As I go to the kitchen, I'm thinking: there's no name on that TV for me. And there never will be. But that's OK—I already have my names. Quint Baker. June Del Toro. Dirk Savage. Rover. Bardle. Even that loony tune Skaelka.

And I have something else.

It sounds a little crazy, even as I say it in my

head—but I have the Slicer. And no, I'm not
getting all Gollum-y.

My blade is not family. It is not *my precious*.
But it is a purpose.

I'm happy now—in our makeshift tree
house kitchen—putting together a big bowl of
movie-watching mix. It's got all the best stuff:
Goobers, Cookie Dough Bites, Sour Patch Kids.

"Put extra Whoppers in!" June shouts, and
I think, *Obviously!* As soon as I return, she's
rushing over to shove her hand into the bowl.

We watch the names until our eyes glaze over. It's past midnight when Quint and June pass out in their beanbag chairs, matching streams of drool dripping from their mouths. I head out onto the tree house deck.

Even out here, I can hear Dirk snoring. His sleep isn't peaceful. He kicks. Tosses. Turns so hard he nearly flips. . . .

All that happiness I felt for Quint and June? It's gone.

Because unless all *four* of us are good—then *none* of us are good. And Dirk is *far* from good.

I grab an armful of soda cans and line them up on the railing. And, for the first time in a long time, I use the Slicer for its intended purpose: whacking the crud out of stuff.

We tried to cheer up Dirk.

But instead we discovered he's worse off than we ever realized. He's not bummed, he's not moping—he is *suffering*.

And not only that, but there's a strange threat out there, looming. The Vine-Thingies have changed, and now they're sucking monsters into the ground. . . .

I pull back the Slicer, swing, and send another soda can flying. It fizzes, soda squirting, as it sails over Joe's Pizza, and then—

"OW!"

A moment later—

IS THIS HOW YOU TRAIN NOW? IS THIS TIN CAN YOUR NEW MENTOR?

I don't want to get into a whole Romeo and Juliet balcony-talking thing, so I climb down from the tree house.

As Bardle crosses the Town Square, I see that he's covered in rat hair and other gunk. Despite that, he's chewing on a pepperoni roll from Joe's. "Any luck learning the secrets of the tail?" I ask.

"I have not yet learned what I hoped to learn."

OK. Super cryptic. But—that's Bardle.

Bardle bites his pepperoni roll—and offers it to me. A small blob of yellow-orange saliva drips from it.

I want to pass.

I've never shared a pepperoni roll with a monster before. I mean, I've never shared a pepperoni roll with *anyone* because trading off bites is the absolute weirdest way to eat a pepperoni roll.

But it's *our* world now. *Shared.*

I take a bite.

"You should be asleep," Bardle says.

"So should you."

Bardle grunts.

"I'm worried about Dirk," I say. "At first, I thought he was weirded out by the zombies 'cause he, y'know, almost was one. But he told me he's hearing weird static, in his head. . . ."

I trail off thinking . . .

A year ago, I didn't even *know* Dirk. But now, if anything happened to him—I don't know what I'd do. He's still here—and I already miss him. . . .

"What about, like, brothers? Sisters? Cousins? Third cousins twice removed?"

"I have 4,932 siblings. I do not know their names, but I know I can defeat nearly all in combat."

"Oh," I say. "OK, that's cool. I guess."

Bardle says, "To feel strongly about a single creature: it is rare. It is not that we are incapable—but it provides no value. If there is no value, what is the reason?"

I frown. "The reason is—well—if I were having FREAK-OUT moments like Dirk, I'd want someone to care enough about me to help. If my brain was, like, breaking and I was falling into weird trances, like when—"

I stop, suddenly realizing what that look on Dirk's face reminded me of. He *looked* like I *felt* when I was hypnotized by the King Wretch.

I'm not sure if Bardle reads my face or my mind or if we're just simpatico, but his eyes flash blue. "The Nightmare King . . ." he says in a gravelly whisper. "Quickly—what is your moon's position?"

"Um. Position? I think it's—above?" Also, I want to explain that it's not technically *my moon*, but eh, what's the point.

"If we go now," Bardle says, "there may still be time. Quickly, retrieve Dirk. And, Jack, one more thing—and this is *absolutely vital* . . ."

I lean forward. "What is it, Bardle?"

"I am chilly. Bring me an item that will make me less chilly."

I grumble an OK, then climb back up the tree house ladder. I gotta tread carefully here. Waking up a sleeping Dirk is *dangerous*—like interrupting a grizzly in the middle of a meal.

I place my hands to the glass—and then too late I remember that our windows don't *have* glass and I tumble in, headfirst, right on top of Dirk.

"So, Bardle," I raise my voice to shout. "Where are we going?"

Bardle turns to me. The sweatpants Dirk lent him are wrapped around his neck, like he's a posh supermodel. The pant-legs whip in the breeze. "To the sea," Bardle says.

Rover carries us farther away from town, his paws galloping in a calming, rhythmic way.

You ever sit in the back of a car on a long

drive? That steady ba-bump of the car—I swear, it is literally the most soothing thing ever.

Maybe it's being an orphan—but sometimes, I feel most at home . . . when I'm moving.

My eyes droop, and I drift off to sleep. . . .

Later—five minutes or five hours, I'm not sure—I wake to a sweet, salty smell. We're stampeding down a boardwalk. I've never been here. We're in far-out Wakefield.

The boardwalk stretches endlessly out in front of us. Oh man, it's like—happiness city. Retro arcades, boogie board stores, and joints that sell fried EVERYTHING.

No zombie beach bums—thankfully. Zombies are freaky enough when fully clothed—I don't need to see them in Speedos.

Rover turns onto a pier that juts straight out across the beach and over the ocean.

This feels like the part in movies where people look out at the ocean and contemplate the vastness of the universe and how we're all like little tiny ants in comparison. But I just look at the ocean now and think, *That water looks cold and it's probably got sharks.*

Rover stops. Bardle climbs out of Dirk's lap and walks to the very edge of the pier.

One more step and he'd drop right into the water.

Bardle's voice is soft. "There is one creature who may be able to tell us what Dirk is experiencing."

Please don't be shark monsters, please don't be shark monsters, please don't be shark monsters.

Bardle waves a hand at Dirk. "What you describe—they sound similar to Jack's visions."

chapter
fifteen

Bardle pulls a stone from his rucksack and lifts it to his lips. A small glob of yellow saliva drops onto it.

He pitches the stone out into the water. I watch to see where it lands, but crashing waves hide the splash.

For a long moment, nothing happens. But then the wooden pier creaks, a chill cuts through me, and the waves go flat. The water is still.

Up above, a large cloud drifts by. It blocks the moon and everything goes dark. When the cloud passes, I gasp.

Something ripples in the water—a football field away. Oh, real quick—a weird thing about me, I don't even really love football, but *any distance*—I measure in football fields. How far is it from here to Arkansas? I dunno—492 football fields?

And then it happens. . . .

I see the creature rising out of the water and it takes all my strength to resist making a break for it. Actually, it takes more than that—

The surging sea creature is so big that the water rushing off its body, smashing the surface, sounds like a rainstorm.

Dirk takes a shaky step backward and stutters, "It's—it's—"

"The Scrapken," I say. "Bardle, the Scrapken tried to kill us!"

"Yes, you have told me the story," Bardle says. "As I understood it, you broke into its home. Destroyed things. Played games atop its head."

"Well, when you say it like that . . ." I mutter. "Also, I don't think we technically *played games atop its head*. It was a sleepover."

It's still rising—the Scrapken is bigger than I ever realized. At the junkyard, *half* of its body must have been buried beneath the ground.

Bardle turns with a grim smile. "Let us make sure the Nightmare King is not playing inside your head, Dirk. The Scrapken, as you call it, always eats what it kills. And the digestive process is slow. . . ."

The Scrapken rises to its full height. One tentacle lifts out of the water and extends toward us, setting its tip down gently on the pier—but the tremendous weight of the thing causes the rickety wood to shift and moan.

The tentacle unfolds outward—like a platform—and there's this feeling like an elevator door is opening.

I've fought ferocious monsters. I've run from undead hordes. This is different.

It feels like this creature was *always* here. I mean, it wasn't—it came through the portals. But it doesn't feel like an *intruder*.

A gentle push at my back. Dirk.

Go.

I think it wants us to, like, go.

How about you first? Y'know, since we're here for your brain? If it was my brain that was being weird, I would totally go first....

BUMP

Dirk mumbles under his breath, then takes a heavy step past me. Argh, now I feel lame. I hurry to keep up. Together, Dirk and I step onto the large flat tentacle.

It's squishy, like standing on a gym mat soaked in sweat. The tentacle dips once more as Bardle steps behind us.

Slowly, we are lifted—the tentacle carrying us out, over the crashing waves, and up toward the creature's mouth and eye.

It's overwhelming. Three small figures standing in the palm of a monster's hand. A monster that could crush, swallow, devour us if it wanted.

Bardle looks nervous, too—not a great sign.

He cracks his knuckles. Not like us—where it's a quick snap or two. It sounds like a hundred bones, cracking like dominoes. Then—

Another tentacle—this one slightly smaller—rises out of the water. It pokes at our bodies, like a dog getting the scent of a new guest.

It prods at Dirk's face. His chest. My head. My shoulder. Around my side, my back, toward—

The Slicer . . .

Suddenly, the tentacle platform roils and we all stagger. Dirk lets out a sharp gasp. I grab Bardle, afraid I might be pitched overboard.

"Bardle," I say, my voice shaky. "I'd like to get off the ride now. I'm not sure I was even tall enough for this ride in the first place."

"Your blade. The Scrapken senses the darkness inside it: Ghazt's power and Ŗeżżőcħ's influence," Bardle says.

FINALLY some clear info from this guy.

"But I'm not bad!" I exclaim. "I'm not, like, in league or in cahoots or in bed—*definitely* not in bed—with Ghazt or Ŗeżżőcħ!"

The Scrapken ROARS—a monstrous explosion of hot air. Its jaw hangs open and I'm afraid we're about to go down the hatch like a handful of mini M&Ms.

"No!" I shout. "I'm not mini M&Ms! And I'm not Ŗeżżőcħ! I'm not a bad dude!"

The tentacle tilts and carries us closer to the

mouth. I squeeze my eyes tight and throw out my hands in defense.

And everything stops.

I open my eyes and see the smaller tentacle snaking around my hand.

It's the hand that's been burned, over and over, by the blade's energy. The Scrapken is studying it.

And—somehow—I think it knows. It understands that I can't wield the blade without injury. Because the blade's essence is tied to cosmic evil. Because it's bad. And I'm not.

And that's when things get really weird. . . .

The tentacle encircles my wrist, wrapping tight, squeezing tighter and tighter like one of those blood pressure things at the doctor. But there's no nurse here to shut it off. . . .

Bardle stands perfectly still, a look on his face like he's enjoying this a little bit.

"Let go of my bud!" Dirk says, and he charges forward. The tentacle only compresses tighter.

"DIRK, NO!" I shout. "STAY BACK!"

The Scrapken seems intent on choking out my arm. But when I look into its humongous eye, it looks sad. Like it's apologizing.

I want to say, "Yeah, I don't like this, either, bud, so feel free to stop at any time!" but my teeth are clenched so tight that I can't speak. I feel pain like I've never felt before, and my eyes close.

I'm seeing stars.

Speckles of light.

Maybe—actual stars?

Other dimensions?

Ŗeżżóch? Cosmic Terrors? The Cosmic Beyond?

I don't know. I just know that I can't take it any longer. For an instant, I feel the blade burning at my back, and I know what I must do. What the Scrapken is *forcing me to do*. . . .

Forcing me to stand.

Forcing me to take my free hand, reach behind my back, grab the Slicer, raise it high.

And I swing—

A quick flurry of chaos. The Scrapken howling. Dirk stammering. Me clutching my arm and shouting up at the monster:

"Sorry! BUT YOU WERE GIVING ME A DEATH TRAP HANDSHAKE, DUDE!"

The severed tentacle waves in front of me, leaking thick blue-green ooze.

But when I look down at my wrist, the other part is still there. On my hand.

My left hand is still gripping the Slicer—and I realize it's burning hot, so I smoothly toss it into my right. There, the tentacle acts like a sort of *glove*—

My gloved hand whips and snaps the Slicer through the air. It responds, nimble and quick, like one of those little fencing swords.

The Scrapken moans in pain—a deep, rumbling wail.

The tentacle platform drops so quick that my stomach does a roller-coaster flip. It sets us back onto the dock. We all take a few steps back, enjoying the solid ground beneath our feet.

"I don't get it," I finally say. "Why would the Scrapken do that? Now *it's* hurt!"

Bardle explains, "Other monsters in this dimension, ones who are not loyal to Ṟeżżőcħ, they sense what is happening, they sense what is to come, and they are on the side of good."

The Scrapken moans and blinks.

"If we are to stop Ṟeżżőcħ, then sacrifices must be made. Great ones. Jack, you made the difficult choice to swing the blade. This creature made the difficult sacrifice of its limb. Do you understand?"

I nod, slowly. "I—I think so."

Suddenly, Dirk pushes forward. "Fine. I get this is, like, a big moment for you guys—but I wanna know *why* I'm hearing stuff in my brain! Is the Nightmare King involved or not?!"

The Scrapken vibrates in the water. Its belly flexes and jiggles. And it answers Dirk's question with a—

PA-TOO!

The Scrapken coughs something up from its belly and spits it onto the pier. Now I know why Bardle said the Scrapken eats what it kills—because the Nightmare King's skull is sliding down the boardwalk.

OK, then . . . Guess the Nightmare King is officially not involved.

The Scrapken lets out a long, low moan—like it's taking its final bow—and slowly slides away, slipping under the water, disappearing beneath the surface.

"Well," I say quietly. "I guess its work here is done. And after what just happened, I'm glad."

We walk back to Rover—all of us trying not to look too closely at the colossal Wretch cranium now sitting near the Flip-and-Fry.

I fiddle with the new tentacle glove. "So, I officially have the coolest winter glove ever. It's like a mitten! But squishy!" Then, after a moment's thought, "Crud, I *always* lose winter gloves."

"I would suggest," Bardle says, "that you do not lose that 'winter glove.'"

I nod. "Gotcha. Loud and clear. I will put it right next to my bed, on top of the comics, behind the Rocketeer Funko, beneath my spare hoodie and my late-night snacking bin, kinda near my collection of old batteries and—"

Dirk suddenly grabs me, spinning me around. His face is pale, his eyes wide—

Jack, if it wasn't the Nightmare King— then **what's wrong with me?**

chapter sixteen

LEGENDARY HERO TRAINING. DAY 19.

Wherein I, Jack Sullivan, use the Squishy Mitten of Power to finally, at last, do some cool zombie manipulation!

OK, here goes. . . .

We're back at the farm, but this time it's gonna be different. I stare down three zombies. "You three better prepare for total domination. I'm comin' for ya with my crazy Scrapken glove!"

I open and close my fingers. The tentacle flesh presses against my thumb.

I pull the Slicer free.

I'm gonna prove my worth.

And then, after all the worth proving, I'm gonna show my friends how *super* good I am at doing zombie-control stuff.

I swing the bat—

"DANCE, UNDEAD ONES! DANCE!" I shout,

snapping the Slicer through the air like
I'm conducting an orchestra or doing some
Sorcerer's Apprentice–style magic.

I feel the magnetic connection and—

I stand there, in total disbelief. Then—

"YOU HAVE GOT TO BE KIDDING ME!" I
scream. "Bardle, what the huh? The Squishy
Mitten of Power didn't work! The zombies just
toppled!"

"Is that what you intend to call it?" Bardle says. "The Squishy Mitten of Power?"

"What? Um, NO. I was just trying it out . . ." I mumble. "Why, do you like it?

"It is horrendous."

"Well, good, 'cause like I said, that's NOT what I'm calling it." I turn and stomp away. Big, heavy, child-tantrum footsteps. I feel the zombies watching me. "Look away, zombies," I whisper angrily. "I don't even wanna see you guys right now, that's how mad I am at you."

I can't control them. I don't know why I thought I could. I'm not Ghazt. I'm not a Cosmic Terror. I'm not even lousy Evie. . . .

Bardle steps toward me. He has a weird shimmer in his eyes like he's about to conjure that horrible terror again.

"No, don't show it to me again," I say. "It's horrible and awful and if I don't do a better job, then everyone is done for. I get it."

I think back to when the Monster Apocalypse began—when I created challenges for myself and earned Feats of Apocalyptic Success.

In those challenges, and in video games, too, when you fail, you can always start again. Even online, in a *Battle Royale*, if you bite it, you just hop into the next game. Easy!

But this—this here—this is like . . .

You fail and the controller melts in your hand—hits the ground, bursts into flames, burns a hole in the floor, and falls through to the netherworld. And while that's happening, lest you thought, *Oh, I'll just go get another controller!* your console spontaneously combusts and then the TV crashes to the floor and explodes in a raging inferno.

Oh yeah—Jack Sullivan. Big hero. I can see it now—my final feat. . . .

FEAT: Complete

FAIL ALL OF HUMANITY.
DISAPPOINT EVERYONE.
BE *NOT* A HERO.

Bardle interrupts my doomsday train of thought, "When you controlled the zombie in the bowling alley—what did you feel?"

"Fear," I say. "I saw that undead eating machine zooming toward Quint, and I was scared."

He nods.

His eyes flick up over my shoulder, and I spin

around—expecting to see a zombie, but there's nothing. Bardle just pulled a "made ya look."

When I turn back, a split second later, he's holding my walkie.

"Hey! How did you—?" I glance around. My backpack, which lies near the fence, is open.

Bardle lifts the walkie, but when his mouth opens, *my voice* comes out. Not, like, an impression of me . . .

My actual voice.

My chest is tight, like Bardle is ripping the words from my throat.

"June. Quint. Dirk. Come in," he says. "It is I, your human companion Jack. I have exciting things to tell you. Out and over."

OK, so he can do my voice—but he's totally butchering my awesome lingo.

"Also, fisticuffs," Bardle says.

Crud. He's good.

"Meet me at the Burger Barn," Bardle says.

A moment later, June replies, "Copy that!"

The Burger Barn is beyond the safety of the Zom-B-Gone torches. There are zombies there. Why would Bardle send my friends into danger?

Then, with horror, I realize . . .

"Bardle, what have you done?!" I glare at him—and then I'm racing toward Rover. I vault over the fence, into his saddle, and we're off.

Rover dashes down the winding path, leaving the farm behind, then through an alleyway between the old baseball card shop and the sneaker store.

I'm speeding through town like a post-apocalyptic Paul Revere: THE ZOMBIES ARE COMING! THE ZOMBIES ARE COMING!

The Burger Barn comes into view.

Big Mama appears in the parking lot, slowing to a stop. The doors open. My friends step out.

In the shadows, behind them, I see yellow eyes glowing. The undead, inching closer. Impending doom.

Still galloping, I grab the Slicer. We speed into the lot. Rover stumbles and I flip over his head.

I swing the Slicer mid-fall and suddenly, I feel it. The glove, the handle of the blade, the hum of otherworldly energy.

A connection.

Between the bat and the zombies.

VRRRRRRUUUUUMMMMMMM!!!

One swing of the blade—a short arc, slicing across my vision, and the zombies are thrown to the ground—

And I land on my butt.

June and Quint stare wide-eyed at the zombies—now lying a couple of feet away. The zombies gaze deeply at the Slicer before rising and wobbling away.

"Jack, what—what was that? What did you do?" June asks.

"You controlled them!" Quint bursts out.

Before I can respond, I realize that Dirk is on the ground. He rubs his head. "Guys, uh—what just happened? I, um . . . collapsed."

June looks at me. Then at the bat. Quint strokes his chin like a professor, which usually means the answer's in his head somewhere, he's just trying to fish it out. But there's no time, because—

"YELP!"

I spin around—Rover! I didn't see it when we rode over—but there's a sinkhole in the ground, at the edge of the alley. Just like the one that was left behind when the Vine-Thingies grabbed the Hairy Eyeball Monster.

Rover is losing his balance, slipping down into the cracked and broken ground.

"Rover!" I cry out, and I'm racing toward him, grabbing his saddle, tugging. "Hang on, buddy!"

"Jack, you'll fall in!" Quint shouts.

June and Quint grab Rover's furry hide and tug. Rover takes slow, heavy steps back. Then, at once, he springs away from the hole.

But the sudden jerk causes me to tumble forward. I see Dirk's meaty paw coming at me, grabbing my ankle, but I'm slipping back. And we're both going over, into the sinkhole, under the earth.

chapter seventeen

Dirk and I tumble through cracked concrete and dirt and down into darkness and then—

WHOMP!

Hard ground.

There's a heavy, wet smell in the air, like soil.

I rise, take a step, then pitch forward into something. Something *alive*. My mouth is open, ready to shriek, but it's Dirk. He throws a big, dirty palm over my face.

"Shh . . ." he says, lifting a finger to his mouth. "These walls have ears—"

"WHAT? *Ears?!*" I scream as I spin, eyes darting, imagining the most horrific thing my mind can conjure: the fabled, long-lost . . .

WALL OF EARS

"No, dingus, not real ears," Dirk says, nodding ahead. "Those. . . ."

I see Vine-Thingies, swaying, bobbing, moving curiously. One snakes toward us, like it's curious.

"I think they're listening to us," Dirk whispers.

"They must know how cool our conversations are."

Dirk jabs me with a quick elbow and nods ahead. Beyond the next cluster of vines, I see endless tunnels.

The only reason we can see at all is because the Vine-Thingies *glow*. They crawl along the tunnel walls, and their flowers hum with purple and green.

"All this neon reminds me of the laser tag joint," I say. "Hey! Idea! After we get outta here, we should—"

"Not now!" Dirk growls, and he steps forward, brushing through a large, pulsating leaf. I follow closely behind.

We turn a corner and it's like someone cranked up the lights on Space Mountain. This isn't just *one* tunnel—it's many tunnels that split and shoot off into forks and branches.

"Whatever carved these tunnels must've been real big," Dirk says as we continue our trek.

Cool air rushes through the tunnel. I pull my hoodie tight.

"Must've done it recently, too," Dirk adds, poking at the wall. "The soil's wet."

Every step on the soft earth squishes beneath our feet. It's quiet, eerily quiet, until—

A spine-chilling SCREAM erupts!

I draw the Slicer. Dirk readies his fists.

We burst around the next corner, ready for anything—

I'm taking you to Jack town!

June fist, right to your nose!

"STOP!" Quint says.

June holds up her armored hand. "Whoa, it's us! Y'know—your friends!"

Fists and Slicer are lowered. "That could have

been messy," June says. "I almost blasted you."

"I'm just happy you're enjoying the Gift," I say with a grin.

Quint points at my arm. "Jack," he says. "You're bleeding."

He's right—a small cut on my arm. Something scraped me as we came around the corner. My eye catches on a spike jutting from the wall.

"Hmm," Dirk says as he plucks it out like a giant splinter.

Quint eyes it. "It's a quill from the Hairy Eyeball Monster." He gives the tunnel a once-over, then adds, "And there are *lots* of them."

The spikey quills fill this section of the tunnel. Some are broken. Others have bits of monster flesh on the end, like they were ripped from the creature's body.

"It's like after the Vine-Thingies captured it, they didn't just beat it up or eat it up," June says.

Quint nods. "They dragged it through here."

"But dragged to where?" I ask.

Dirk extends his arm, drops the quill, and it hits the dirt floor with a muffled thud. Then it rolls down the path like a runaway pencil.

"We've been going down this whole time," Quint says.

June nods ahead. "Then we keep going down."

The more we walk, the more the tunnel twists and turns. We're on a winding, spiraling path down into the earth deep beneath Wakefield.

"My ears just popped," I say. "Anyone got any Bubblicious?"

"Shh!" Dirk says. "Movement up ahead."

We all stop to listen. At first, it sounds like slithering. Then it's like clicking and clacking. . . .

I poke Dirk. "See, buddy! You remember *Ghostbusters* quotes. Your brain can't be broken if you're quoting *Ghostbusters*. In fact, that probably means you're firing on all cylinders."

"Nah," Dirk grunts. "If I'm quoting movies like you dorks, my brain might be *shattered*."

The clicking, clacking, slithering sound grows louder. And then something else.

"Moaning," June says.

Quint shakes his head. "No. Wailing."

The tunnel flattens out and I see light around the next curve. We've come to the end.

A curtain of tangled vines hangs over the gaping mouth of the passageway. Neon, spectral light glows beyond it.

"OK," I say, looking at my buds. "Just gonna throw this out there. . . . We *could* turn around, and just forget we ever came down here. Go back to the tree house, get some peanut butter sandwiches going, maybe a little cartoon marathon?"

Dirk bravely brushes aside the draping vines.
We step through the curtain, and part of me
wishes we *had* gone back.

And not just because I love a good peanut
butter sandwich cartoon marathon.

Because what we see before us . . .

It's a graveyard.

chapter eighteen

No one speaks for a long, long moment. I can almost feel the terror and fear coming from my friends.

We are in a stunningly huge cavern, and what's inside is ghastly. Grisly. There's a quick jerking in my chest—my heart skipping wildly.

There are monsters everywhere. They're scattered across the cavern floor like peanut shells at a baseball game. Like scraps of garbage, like leftovers, like Starburst wrappers. The ground is *covered* with barely breathing beasts.

"I think some are dying . . ." June whispers.

"And some are already dead," Dirk says softly.

As my eyes adjust to the dim, strange light, it only gets worse. And worse. . . .

We slip down to the cavern floor, not quite believing what we see as we take in the spectacle.

All these creatures are shriveled and shrunken.

You ever suck down a Capri Sun, squash it in your hands, and toss it?

That's what this is like. . . .

Except these aren't juice boxes—they are living creatures. Monsters, yes. But not *evil* monsters. No Dozers or Winged Wretches.

"So many creatures," I say softly. "I see ones we haven't seen since we were tracking down monsters for the bestiary."

Quint smiles wistfully. "Ah, the bestiary. Some of our finest work."

Quint and June kneel down to examine one moaning creature while Dirk inspects the Vine-Thingies. I step toward a monster I recognize: the Hairy Eyeball Monster.

"Hey, buddy," I say, "Long time, no see."

I realize its eye—*its body*—is glazed over and I add, "Sorry, didn't mean it like that—'no see' like an eyeball joke. My bad."

"It's in bad shape," Dirk says, coming up behind me.

The eyeball—splitting, sucking, closing—
reminds me of a goldfish, yanked from its tank,
gasping for water.

Dirk says, "The Vine-Thingies—they're plugged
into its body, like baby cows sucking on the
mama."

Looking around, I see it's the same for every
single monster in the place. My eyes follow the
thick, tube-like vines. They lead away from
the creatures and across the cavern floor like
crisscrossing electrical wires.

The snarled mess of vines meet at the far side
of the cavern. There's a huge, sloping wall—and
the vines grow up it. They thicken as they near
the ceiling, turning nearly black.

There's a smell in the air.

A chemical smell. Weed killer . . .

The same stuff we used to blow up Thrull the Tree Beast. And that's when it hits me.

"Guys, I get it!" I suddenly say, and the thing I "get" makes me want to hurl. "I know *exactly* where we."

"Jack," Quint sighs. "You definitely do *not* know exactly where we are. We've walked nearly a mile underground. And you have a terrible sense of direction. . . ."

"Do not!" I say as I whirl around—

I have a great sense of direction, Quint!

Over here, bud.

I spin back around the other way. "Whoops. OK, fine, my sense of direction is crummy. But I'm *not* wrong! We're beneath the Tree of Entry. That's why these Vine-Thingies are extra super thick. They're not just vines—they're *roots*."

We look around, our eyes tracing the Vine-Thingies to the roof of the cavern. There, the roots of the Tree of Entry come together in one massive knot. Like a big overhead light.

I'm suddenly overwhelmed by the awful feeling that we're trespassing—that we are inside some foul thing's lair.

But who or what?

I look away from the knotted root in the ceiling and follow the thickest vines down, along the far wall. I notice that they twitch and jump, their coils tightening around the helpless monsters in the graveyard. They're connected to something—something that is up there, on the wall.

Something that is, like, cocooned.

Squinting, I step forward. And I see him.

A face I had hoped to never see again.

Thrull. . . .

His name beats in my head like a drum. Thrull. Thrull. Thrull.

I thought we *defeated him*.

He was gone. . . .

June whispers, "It's like he's trapped there."

Quint nods. "An insect in the spider's web."

Thrull's body glows with the same neon as the Vine-Thingies. And every time the vines snap and jump, Thrull's body trembles.

I shake my head. "I don't think he's trapped. I think he's in control."

There's a moment where the fear breaks—and we use it to take cover. We duck behind a large monster that reminds me of a beetle, on its back. Long, thin legs stick out. Black paste drips from its wide, round mouth.

June hmms. "The Tree of Entry *fed* on zombies—that's how it grew to became the door for Ŗeżżőcħ."

"Look around," Dirk says. "All these monsters. You think maybe—maybe Thrull's been feeding on *them* . . . ?"

I peek around the corner. The vines vibrate and shiver with Thrull's every breath. I can barely tell where the vines stop and his humanoid monster figure begins.

I whisper. "It's almost like the vines are *carrying* life into his body. To revive him. Reanimate him."

"When Thrull became Thrull the Tree Beast," Quint says, "he must have become linked to the plants. We destroyed the tree—but not its roots."

I gulp. It makes sense—in that strange way things make sense these days.

Thrull wasn't gone. He didn't just fade away.

He was pulled into the ground.

And he's been down here ever since.

It's at that moment—as I have that horrible realization—that Thrull's eyes flash open.

I almost hear the sound—a scary movie BOOM as he comes to life. It's like he's emerging from hibernation.

Vines snap, bark breaks, and Thrull begins to move. Like if a tree were to stretch its limbs.

Then I hear something totally, entirely different—and totally, entirely unexpected.

The old *Spider-Man* theme.

"Um . . . does anyone else hear whistling?" June asks.

"Who could whistle in an awful place like this?!" Quint exclaims.

I know *exactly* what sort of crazy-pants could whistle in a creepy terror cavern. Coming through another vine-cut tunnel is Evie Snark.

We crouch behind the heaving monster body. "What's she doing here?" June hisses.

Dirk whispers, "I guess she made it out of the sewer."

"Evie and Thrull must be in cahoots!" I say. "Big-time cahoots. Major-league cahoots! I bet they got their own Mission Operation thing going. Mission Operation: Cahoots."

June flicks my wrist. "Stop saying all those things."

"Look!" Quint says. "Thrull's moving. . . ."

Thrull's voice is wet and phlegmy. The vines and tentacles tremble with each word. "I will speak with no human. I will—"

"Ghazt," Evie interrupts. "Ghazt the General sent me."

"Ghazt . . . He is here? In this dimension?" Thrull croaks. "How?"

"I summoned him."

"Remarkable. Ghazt is a great Servant. So, the Tower is well underway, I assume. . . ."

Evie pauses. Coughs into her hand. "Tower? Um. No. Actually, Ghazt's real focus right now is, um . . . nachos. . . ."

Thrull shifts. "What are these—nachos that you speak of?

"Um. Chips and cheese and sometimes, like, different meats and—actually, y'know, it's not super important right now. See, when Ghazt came to this dimension, there were issues. He didn't enter a human vessel. He entered a, ah, rodent. Now his tail is the organ that controls the undead. Or, it did. Some kids and their monster friends . . . they stole his tail. . . ."

Thrull growls, "Kids?"

"Small humans."

Thrull's face contorts. "Were there four?"

Evie nods.

"Head in the game, guys!" June says.
"They're saying important stuff!"

"But Ghazt has made no mention of the Tower?" Thrull asks, and he sounds confused.

I look at my friends—and we all mouth the word. "Tower?"

"Probably bad, right?" I say.

"Not a good tower," June says. "It's for sure not like an inflatable, bouncy birthday party tower."

"Pay attention and maybe we'll find out," Dirk mutters.

"No," Evie says softly. "No mention of the Tower."

Thrull smiles. "Then Ghazt has told you nothing of consequence."

Those words—and Evie's frustration at them—hang heavy in the cavern.

Thrull explains, "As you surely know, Ghazt is the general—and the Tower is his greatest weapon. It is a *beacon*. It beckons the general's soldiers—the undead—drawing them from across the lands to aid in its construction."

Evie goes still.

"When fully complete, the Tower will carry Reżżőch here. The Tower is indomitable, unstoppable transportation to any dimension." A dark, cruel grin grows on Thrull's face. "If the tail is the key to Ghazt building his army and constructing the Tower, I will help you retrieve it. *For Ghazt. For Reżżőch.*"

I whirl to look at my friends. All our eyes are wide as saucers. I can't believe Evie asked Thrull to help Ghazt! More important—I can't believe Thrull *agreed*! And it all has to do with the tail. . . .

Thrull growls, "But first—we must deal with these—little humans."

I just about swallow my tongue. "You guys, I think he knows we're here."

Thrull's body stiffens, and the vines connecting him to the wall suddenly *snap!*

The gray monster we're hiding behind quakes. Its body ripples and swells, like there's soda bubbling beneath its skin.

"It's still alive?" I whisper.

"Or coming back to life," June says. "Like Frankenstein?"

"You mean Frankenstein's *monster*," Quint says. "Frankenstein is the *man*."

"Frankenstein isn't *the man*!" I say. "He's a big lumbering terror creature! How does that make him *the man*?"

"I don't mean he's the man like he's *awesome*. I mean he's the *human* character in the story!"

"Guys," Dirk growls. "SHUT. UP. NOW."

A shadow passes beneath the gray monster's skin. The vines. They're coming out. . . .

"Get back!" Quint shouts, and then—

SCHLA-BOOM!

All at once, exploding monster guts and erupting vines are *everywhere*. It's like an exploding monster guts and erupting vines convention!

Vine-Thingies blast out of the limp monster remains strewn across the graveyard.

BOOM! POP! PA-POP!

The speeding vines reach for us, snaking closer, trying to stop us. . . .

"This way!" June shouts. She leads us on a mad dash back toward the tunnel we came from.

Steel flashes in the air as she uses the Gift's Wolverine-style blade to slice through vines. Green goo splatters the ground. "Don't let 'em get hold of you!" she shouts.

"They'll suck your insides out!" Quint cries. "Just like these vacuum-sucked creatures!"

I hop over one creature, trip on the next, stagger over another.

This is like the obstacle course during that one really good week of gym class!

But a lot more, ugh, damp. . . .

And deadly!

We just need to make it back to the maze of winding tunnels. In front of me, June, Dirk, and Quint disappear through one earthy doorway. I'm springing for it when—

A booming voice stops me.

For a second, it's like there are speakers in my head—like I'm being hypnotized. But then it's coming from *everywhere*. Surround sound.

It's Thrull.

I turn. I don't want to, but I can't help myself.

Across the cavern, I see him, up in his cocoon.

Evie's down below, beneath him, like the teacher's pet. Only this teacher's pet is plenty villainous on her own.

KRAK-KA-KA-KAA-KRAKKKKK

High above, the roots of the Tree of Entry— all that remains of it—begin weaving together. Hundreds upon hundreds, intertwining.

They're forming one twisted, sinewy thing so mega-massive that it makes me think of a runaway freight train. . . .

Now I know what dug these massive tunnels: this tremendous drill bit creature.

It bends toward me, flashing neon like a strobe light. Then it detaches from the ceiling and drops, belly flopping to the cavern floor, flattening anything beneath it.

Its "head" rises.

It is . . .

- THE TENDRILL! -

Thousands of slithering, pulsing vines—like live spaghetti.

Body mass filled with dead or dying monsters.

Drill bit maw, for devastatingly deadly digging!

It's horrifying. But not as horrifying as Thrull, because he's coming. He's descending the wall. The vines hand him off, cradling him down from branch to branch.

Thrull might not be all the way healed— but he's jailbreaking out of that cocoon.

My eyes are locked on his.

Thankfully, Quint's there, pulling me into the tunnel, shouting, "Come, friend!"

And just in time, because the Tendrill is driving across the cavern toward me.

chapter nineteen

The chasing Tendrill fills the tunnel entirely.
Pebbles and soil rain down on us.

"I don't like the way the plants are flickering

like horror movie bathroom light bulbs!" June shouts.

I slip on a mound of soil, face-plant into the ground, then get back up. "Guys!" I shout. I'm screaming at the top of my lungs, but the Tendrill is louder. "It's not just . . . the Vine-Thingies . . . it's bigger! The Tendrill."

My friends dash around the next turn. I tuck in my head and run faster. Speeding after them, I holler, "GUYS! IT'S BIG! REALLY BIG!"

"How big?" Dirk shouts as he glances back. His eyes go scary wide. "Oh. *That* big."

Up ahead, June seems to somehow find another gear—and picks up speed. We're going uphill the entire way.

I've got a cramp in my side like I swallowed a ninja star and it got wedged in the side of my gut. Unfortunately for us, I bet the Tendrill doesn't even *get* cramps. Lucky no-cramp-getting tendrill with two Ls.

"Look! More quills!" Quint calls out, pointing up ahead.

"That means go left!" Dirk says. "That's the way we came!"

We're nearly to the surface.

But the Tendrill is close—and getting closer.

"I'm gonna try to slow the thing down!" I shout,
as I yank the Slicer from over my shoulder.

I plunge it into the tunnel wall, dragging it
through the dirt as I run. I twist the handle, soil
spills out, and soon the tunnel wall is *collapsing*
behind us.

"Faster, faster, faster!" I cry.

Another turn—then I catch sight of the crater where we entered. A rope dangles through a hole in the surface—Big Mama's tow cable.

June leaps for the rope.

Quint's behind her, sailing toward it.

Dirk grabs hold.

They're being lifted up. At the last instant, I jump. Dirk grabs my wrist.

"Pull me!" I cry.

"Pulling, bro!"

And then a final YANK and I'm exploding out of the dirt. Dirk races toward Big Mama. Then—

KAAA-VOOSH!

The Tendrill ERUPTS through the ground, radiating like an earthquake. The monster's surging body is like a whale breaching the surface. The sharp, fringed head of the Tendrill screeches in anger.

"It's like an extension of Thrull," Quint says. "Doing his bidding."

"I am SO not cool with that," June snarls.

"GET IT!!!" I shout, and June, Quint, Rover, and I spring forward to attack. . . .

The Tendrill wails! It sways from side to side like an out-of-control garden hose. Goo sputters out like a sprinkler. Then—

CA-CLINK.

Looking back, I see Dirk at the wheel of Big Mama, with a mean, hard look in his eyes.

It's a look that says: "I'm Dirk Savage. I've been bitten by a zombie and survived—and I've got weirdness in my brain but I'm still going—and I've pretty much got nothing left to lose, so BRING IT."

His hand slaps down, Big Mama lurches, and—

KA-BOOM!

Goo-slime grenades! Smash-crash candles! All launching through the air, aimed to strike!

But before they hit, the Tendrill squirms back beneath the ground. The rockets whistle past us and land harmlessly somewhere in the distance.

The Tendrill escaped.

And now the drumming in my head returns, except this time it's saying—

Thrull. Is. Back. Thrull. Is. Back.

"We have to speak with Bardle," Quint says.

I nod. "We have to get rid of that tail. Now."

chapter twenty

Dandy-Lions ice cream parlor is near the edge of town. There's not much nearby: a gas station, a handful of trees, and a T. J. Maxx parking lot.

Rain is beating down hard, pouring sideways in sheets.

We park Big Mama around the back, then race for the entrance.

I push through the doors—and I'm instantly punched in the nose by a putrid sour milk stench. Turns out, year-old ice cream does *not* smell the best. Who knew?

Stale waffle cones crack beneath my feet like broken glass.

"Quint, this is where you and Bardle do your, like, tail research?" June asks.

"It's gross and weird," Quint admits. "But there's free Oreo crumble!"

The tail is in the center of the shop, atop a metal table. It's hard to believe this shriveled rat tail—with pieces of melted action-figure plastic inside—is the key to controlling and activating *an army of total undead terror.*

Bardle stands over the tail, pondering.

"Bardle," I say breathlessly. "Thrull is back."

The light reflecting off the table colors his face a ghostly yellow-white. Rain whips in and the wind slams the door shut. Thunder rumbles in the distance. Drops of water seep through the ceiling.

Bardle looks like a mad scientist as he turns to us. "I know," he says. "And he wants the tail."

Quint exclaims, "We have to—"

Quint, confused: "What?"

Bardle sags. "Quint, I knew from the start that no good could come of the tail. But I hoped your research might reveal a weakness. However, it seems an impossible feat. All that I've tried has made *me* weak."

"But we have to," I say. "Thrull will—"

But I pause before I can finish.

Because it's eerily quiet all of a sudden—and somehow, I know it's Thrull.

He's here.

His voice booms louder than thunder.

"I HAVE COME FOR THE TAIL!"

I look to my friends. We all have the same frozen expression on our faces: fear, questioning. What's next? What do we do?

I move to the drive-thru window—and I see that he's not alone.

I slide the window shut. It knocks over an old tip jar, and coins roll out, clanging against the wet pavement. Way to go, Jack. Super smooth.

It's not like a tiny plastic window is gonna keep us safe from what's out there, but still. It's *something*.

Dirk grunts, "Feels like the Old West in here. We're holed up in this ice cream parlor like it's a shack on the plains—and Thrull's the black-hatted bandit outside."

My eyes scan the store. "We gotta do something, or this ice cream parlor shack is gonna be our tomb."

Bardle's face is blank, but his lips are moving—whispering to himself. It's like he's working something out in his head.

Finally, he nods—slow and heavy. "There is one thing I can attempt. Please, step back. . . ."

Bardle places his hands on the tail. His eyes close, and the atmosphere seems to change.

The air around us starts to glow.

The pounding rain—like horrible vampire fingernails tap-tap-tapping the roof—intensifies.

Wind whooshes and whips. I grab on to a nearby table, suddenly afraid that I'm gonna be yanked into a tornado destined for who-knows-where.

Bardle shudders and the knotted tail throbs and swells. Thousands of thick, terrible hairs stand on end.

He's doing it! Bardle's doing it!
Everything is going to be—

SLAM!

The door flies open. Thrull's shadow looms in the doorframe. He grips his war hammer.

Bardle looks up. He doesn't run. Instead, he turns to ME and—

The tail glows. Bardle jerks. I feel a strange, brief *zap*—like touching a doorknob after walking across the carpet in socks.

Bardle releases me.

I stumble back as Thrull swings.

KRAK!!!

There is a flash of light. Heat washes over me.

I fly back, through a wall—but I don't feel it.

And then I'm lying on the pavement, in the parking lot, flat on my butt.

There's ringing in my ears like Christmas bells.

The flash of light left an afterimage—if I shut my eyes tight, I can see it: Thrull swinging his hammer downward.

Sitting up, I rub my eyes. It's too dark to make out much from the parking lot, but I see that all four walls of the ice cream parlor are gone.

Somehow, the metal table at the center of the room still stands, with the tail resting on top. The giant plastic soft serve cone that was perched atop the roof is now on its side, cracked and caved in.

Evie stands in the rain, like a statue, watching.

I whip my head around, searching for my friends. They were beside me, before. . . .

"Guys?" I call out. "You OK?"

I hear a groan from the trees. June. "Never better . . ." she manages.

From across the way, Dirk says, "Peachy."

And then Quint's voice: "I'm fine, friends."

Knowing they're OK—that gives me a little strength. I try to stand—but immediately slip. My chin scrapes the cement and pebbles slice their way into my palm.

I reach out with the glove hand and the suction-cup grip steadies me.

Ash and debris is everywhere, but there's something else . . . rainbow sprinkles. They mix with the rain and fall like confetti. It's the only bright thing in this sea of darkness.

The smoke clears, and through the pink-and-yellow-and-red-sprinkle drizzle I see two figures.

Bardle: on one knee, slowly and shakily rising.

Thrull: towering over him.

Thrull's voice drifts across the parking lot. "I
see Jack's blade has changed. The human, Evie,
says he can manipulate the undead. And his hand
is now a cosmic glove . . . Bardle, you have been
up to a great deal while I slept. A teacher?
A guide? Is that what you think you are?"

Bardle says nothing.

Thrull snarls. "This is not your world, Bardle.
Why do you care? You have grown soft here. Our
kind—we do not feel for others. . . ."

Bardle reaches down and shakily draws his
sword.

"I am not eager to do this," Thrull says.

Bardle is silent.

"You failed," Thrull says, and his voice is gruff and scornful. "The tail will be mine. CONTROL will be mine. But I do not need to destroy you."

Bardle—slowed, weakened—raises his sword. Thrull nods. "If that is what you prefer. . . ."

My eyes are watering, so what happens next is blurred. I'm thankful for that.

Thrull lifts the war hammer and it seems to hang in the air, defying gravity, then he swings—

A crashing boom. A flash of energy. And then metal crunching—Bardle slamming into a nearby car. Thrull's blow catapulted him out of the wreckage and across the street.

I scramble to Bardle's side. His clothes are torn. But he doesn't look—y'know—*dead*. I mean, a big war hammer swings into your buddy's body—you expect to see the worst.

"Bardle, you're OK!" I say. "Holy crud, that scared me! OK, we gotta get outta here. Now."

Bardle's eyes narrow—and I follow his gaze. Inside the store's crumbling shell, Thrull is hunched over the tail like he's about to devour it. He extends his not-yet-healed arm, exposing little tendrils of flapping flesh.

Bardle's heavy-lidded eyes squint up at me. "Jack," he says. "I am not OK. My energy absorbed the hammer's blow. But I am now weakened . . . beyond mending. . . ."

Bardle still grips the handle of his sword—but reaches out for me with his free hand. "Jack . . ." he says. His voice is soft and thin. "The power to control—it can be yours entirely. But—it is—it is . . ."

"What?" I kneel over Bardle, taking his hand. "Bardle! I don't understand! Help me understand!"

He squeezes my hand before uttering weakly,
"It is your choice, Jack. But it is a tremendous
burden. And for that, I am so very sorry. . . ."

"Sorry? For what?"

Bardle's head turns up. He's trying to say
more—trying to tell me everything he can. But
his body shivers and he only manages—

Bardle's long fingers tighten around mine. He's so weak that I barely feel the squeeze beneath my glove.

His lips open, like he wants to say one last thing. But he can't. His mouth is a sagging, lopsided O.

His sword clangs to the pavement.

His half-open eyes are dull and pale.

Then, they close.

And that—that's how it happens.

That's how Bardle dies.

chapter twenty-one

Thick, melted ice cream is splattered in a sticky layer across the ground, dotted with rainbow sprinkles. It looks like the world was hit by a cake batter cyclone.

Through the rain, I see Thrull. . . .

He jams his fleshy, flapping arm into the cut-open side of the tail—

The tail fuses with Thrull's arm, forming one long, terrifying appendage. Of course he wasn't going to return the tail to Ghazt. He wanted zombie control for himself. And now he has it. . . .

He's a liar.

I learned that the hard way.

Now Evie has, too. Out of the corner of my eye, I see her backing away, out of sight.

The tail twists, turning Thrull. His back is to me. So I rise and begin to cross the parking lot.

But I'm too scared to confront him. And too angry to do nothing.

The rain comes down in buckets.

Before I can decide—

Rover's carrying me in his mouth like a lion cub and Big Mama is whipping toward us. June's at the wheel. Quint beside her, Dirk in the back.

They're all OK.

I don't breathe a sigh of relief—but, yeah, a tiny bit of relieved nose breath shoots out my nostrils.

"What are we doing?" I ask as Rover races up beside Big Mama.

"Fleeing!" Quint shouts.

"But, Bardle!" I cry. "We can't leave him!"

"We gotta," Dirk says. "For now."

I don't know how to respond to that. But then Rover leaps up, into Big Mama's truck bed. I guess I'd rather be out of the cold, so I crawl through the rear window, inside, to my friends.

Quint pulls me close, and I'm happy—happy the rain is there to hide my tears. . . .

chapter twenty-two

Big Mama speeds toward the Christmas tree farm. But I'm just in a daze, ignoring the world racing by. I wish I was somewhere else. I wish I was *someone* else—someone who didn't just see what I saw. . . .

Bardle's body, lying there. . . .

I feel a hand on my arm. Quint. He says, "I know, Jack. I know."

I want to scream, "NO! You DON'T know!"

But I say nothing.

I look out, at the trees and buildings racing by. At the Vine-Thingies crawling over everything. This invasion of other-dimensional evil . . .

I shut my eyes tight and as I do, I hear Bardle's voice. But it's not my imagination. It's not something mystic. The voice is *real*. Somehow, Bardle is speaking to me.

From the beyond . . .

The voice says, "You must remain strong, Jack. You must, because . . ."

"Quint!" I howl. "I'm in mourning! What are you doing??"

"An Obi-Wan thing!"

"Now is *not* the time for an Obi-Wan thing!"

"I'm sorry!" Quint says. "Emotional situations make me uncomfortable and I don't know what to do! But I do believe humor can heal even the biggest wounds!"

I turn toward the window to sulk in peace when my heart just about jumps into my throat. Big Mama's tires are squealing, the brakes screeching, and we're jolting forward.

Something is moving in the road.

Warg.

Her hundreds of eyeballs glow as the headlights flash over her.

I jump from the truck. The door echoes in the quiet night. Behind me, June says, "Warg? What are you doing here? We were going to the farm—"

"It's too late," Warg says.

"What?"

"Thrull came," she says. "He took them. The zombies. An enormous plant creature made of roots and vines erupted from the soil."

"The Tendrill," I growl. "The Tendrill with two Ls."

"The zombies are gone," Warg says. "Every last one. . . ."

Warg's eyes zoom in all directions, searching. Then they narrow their focus on me. Warg quietly asks, "Where is Bardle?"

I open my mouth to tell her, "He's gone," and the next second, water begins to pool beneath her body. Every single eyeball leaks tears, forming a puddle so big it might just flood the whole street.

It's Dirk who kneels down over her and says, "Come on. Let's get you to the tree house."

chapter
twenty-three

We roll past Joe's Pizza. The windows glow
and music drifts into the streets. Our monster
friends don't know what it's like to grieve.

At the tree house, we all help Warg up, inside.

She settles into a chair. It's my gaming chair—
the RollMaster781—and she perches on it in a
strange, cartoonish way. One by one, her eyes
blink open, on and off like twinkling Christmas
bulbs.

She looks around, her body of eyes scanning
the tree house. "What is this place?"

"Our home," I say.

Dirk chuckles in a soft, sad way. "Welcome to
the tree house at the end of the world. . . ."

"Let's get her some water," June says to Quint.
"Wait, do the monsters drink water?"

"I think so," Quint says. "Although, I've never
actually seen any partake in H_2O."

"She's gotta replenish all those tears, right?"
June says. "She *must* be dehydrated."

I whirl around. My hands are shaking. "GUYS! Just get *something*!"

June and Quint hurry to Quint's room, where he keeps his gadgets and science-y things.

My head hangs—staring down at my sneakers for a long, long time. Finally, I look up at Warg.

"I don't understand," I say, and I'm not sure if I'm angry or just confused. "I thought you didn't care about anyone? You live up on the farm, all alone. . . . Why do you get to be sad?"

IT IS EXACTLY *BECAUSE* I CARE THAT I HAVE ISOLATED MYSELF.

THAT CARING— IT IS A FLAW IN MY BEING. DO YOU KNOW HOW IT FEELS TO GROW ATTACHED TO A CREATURE WHO CANNOT GROW ATTACHED IN RETURN?

After a long moment, I quietly say, "Oh."

"And now you know my secret," Warg whispers.

"This whole time we just thought you were a big grumper," Dirk says.

That's when we hear June scream.

A moment later, she appears in the doorway. Her face is part shock, part crazy-pants excitement.

And then Quint is there, too. A TV is cradled in his arms, the cord snaking around his leg—he's attempting to rush into the room with it. But the TV doesn't fit through the doorway and there's a *smack* when it bangs into the wall, sending him tumbling back.

"Ahem," he says, readjusting himself. He tries walking in backward, but the TV is still just as wide. Another *smack*. He finally sneaks through sideways, and when he turns around, I see . . .

Whoa.

The TV recording is paused. But there, on the screen, I see—

June's parents. Their names.

"It worked," she says breathlessly. "They're OK. My parents are OK—and they're out there somewhere. . . ."

I look to Quint. "And . . . and yours, buddy?"

He blinks quickly. He's chewing on his lip. "I don't know. I'm—I'm too scared to look. It's recorded. I just need to rewind. But I'm not sure if . . ." His voice trails off and his eyes drift away from us.

I swallow and decide this is a best friend's job. Like ripping off the Band-Aid.

I press the REWIND button. Thousands of names speed in reverse. It's like watching a Star Wars opening scrawl, but upside down.

We stand, all of us in silence, for some of the longest minutes of my life. And then—

I see the name.

Baker.

Then—oh no—another Baker.

And another.

"Quint, there are, like, a gajillion Bakers! Why do you gotta have such a popular last name?!"

"JACK, C'MON!" Quint shouts.

The names creep past, slower, and then I pause.

I swallow. There's a lump in my throat.

His mom. His dad.

I see their names.

And I say, with a smile, "If I was a lousy friend, I could mess with you *so hard* right now. . . ."

Quint's eyes shine and glow with a wetness that he has to blink away.

It's happiness. Insane, unbelievable happiness. It bubbles over so much that I just throw my arms around Quint and June, but there's the darn TV, which is too big to allow for a real group hug, so it ends with me just kind of hugging the screen.

Then I feel Dirk's arms wrapped around us as wide as they can go.

And for minutes—minutes and minutes and minutes—we just hold each other and say nothing.

It's sorta the grand finale of so much: the radio, the King Wretch, June's hopes and wants, my fears and worries, and that first day I found Quint and we hung out in his oddly quiet house, because his parents were gone and he didn't want to say anything more about it and—

"I GET IT!" Quint suddenly exclaims. He says it so loudly that we're all practically thrown backward. "Dirk, I know what's wrong with you!"

Dirk takes a step back. "You do?"

Quint nods. "It's just like Warg! Just like this TV!"

Quint's mind has made a sudden leap into new territory, and I have whiplash.

He launches into an explanation and his arms start waving wildly—until he remembers he's still holding the TV. He nearly drops it three times before saying, "June, uh, would you mind?"

June wordlessly takes the TV from Quint. She leans it against the couch and runs her hand over the names. I can tell she wants to rewind and see her parents' names again.

"Warg," Quint says, walking over to her.

"When we first met you, your eyeballs swarmed around us. They *each* did something different, but they are all an extension of *you*. How does that work?"

Warg's eyeballs jiggle. A few jump off her body and roll around on the floor, which is *super dirty*—those eyeballs are definitely picking up some Kit Kat crumbs.

Warg's body shrugs. "I think a thought, and the eyeballs communicate the thought to one another. It simply works."

Quint says, "Like a hive mind!"

What is a hive mind?! What does this mean?!

I just want to know why my head sounds like freaking zombie radio!

"Look," Quint says. "Jack and I have seen every zombie movie ever made—and I don't remember *any* in which zombies fought on *command*."

"That *is* true," I say.

Quint continues, "So, these things we call zombies—they aren't *just* zombies. I mean, they *are*, but there's *more* to them. Don't forget, the zombie plague originated in another dimension—it may not follow the usual Earthly rules. . . ."

Dirk sighs so heavily that the tree house walls just about shake.

"What does an interdimensional zombie plague have to do with a hive mind and what does that have to do with me HEARING WEIRD STUFF??"

"Quint, buddy," I say quietly in his ear. "Maybe get to the part where you tell Dirk what's up with his noggin?"

"Right, certainly, of course!" Quint says. "Dirk, you were nearly zombified—but the process was stopped before completion. But I believe there was an aftereffect of that near-transformation: you are now connected to the zombie hive mind—but *just barely*."

"Oh. Right . . ." Quint says. "Of course, it's not exciting for you, Dirk, but it is—"

"Bad," Dirk says. "It's only bad."

"Hold on," I say to Dirk. "Maybe it's *not* bad. FOR REAL. I mean, now that we know what's wrong, we can figure out how to make it better!"

"Indeed," Quint says. "The closer you are to the zombies, the stronger the connection. So you just gotta stay away from them!"

"Right, right, this is all GREAT news," Dirk says, his voice all angry sarcasm. "Who *wouldn't* be happy to find out they're connected to zombies, right? So, really—everyone's happy. You two are happy your parents are OK, and—"

The sound of breaking glass silences Dirk. We all spin—the huge flat-screen TV is on the floor. A crack runs through it. June's eyes are narrowed and she's loading goo-slime cans into the Gift.

LISTEN UP!

None of this matters if Thrull builds the Tower.

You heard what he said: it's unstoppable. Rezzóch will come.

Won't matter that our parents are alive.

Won't matter if Dirk gets better.

And if we don't steal back the zombies, Thrull's gonna have one major head start on building that thing. . . .

"We don't even know where Thrull is," Quint says. "Or the zombies. Or Evie and Ghazt."

We sit there. The thick feeling of hopelessness settling in.

That's when Dirk stands. "But maybe we can find out," he says. "The TV, the Wi-Fi, the video game. They pick up signals in the air, right?"

Quint thinks. "In the air? Um. Well—I suppose, yes. Though that's a very simplified explanation."

"And I pick up signals from the zombies, right? Kinda?" Dirk asks.

Quint nods. Everyone's silent, waiting for Dirk to continue.

"Well, what I hear—it's fuzzy. It's not *clear*. But maybe if I got closer to the zombies, it *would* be clear. And if I *could* hear . . ."

"You would know what the zombies know," Quint finishes for him. "You'd know what Thrull's doing."

"But, Dirk," I say. "When you get near the zombies—"

"It hurts," he says with a resigned shrug. "But sometimes you gotta take one for the team. And you guys—you're my team."

chapter twenty-four

The next few minutes unfold faster than fast. Mission Operation: Cheer Up Dirk has morphed into Mission Operation: Dirk and the Great Zombie Hive Mind. And it's all hands on deck.

The Wi-Fi's satellite dish is loaded into Big Mama.

Quint's football helmet—the one he was using to try to pick up the tail's energy—goes on Dirk's head.

The helmet connects to Big Mama's stereo.

Car keys go into the ignition.

Dirk lies down in Big Mama's truck bed. Quint sits beside him, strapped into the seat, the satellite nearby.

"You guys ready?" I ask.

Dirk and Quint nod.

Inside Big Mama's glove box is a map of Wakefield and the surrounding area. I'm unfolding it as June says, "I'll drive."

And I don't argue, 'cause it's an argument I'd lose. Partly 'cause June's got a bone to pick with the Tower that's threatening the family she just found out is still alive. And partly 'cause I'm a lousy driver.

"Good luck," Warg says. She stands outside the tree house, with Rover at her side.

And then the keys are turning and the engine is roaring and we're all just hoping. . . .

We drive and drive. June steers us in a spiral, starting at the tree house, then spreading out like a pinwheel, wider and wider, so we don't miss anything.

It's like holding up your cell phone, hoping for enough bars to make a call to get a ride home from soccer practice. Except, Dirk's head is the phone and this call is the key to *everything*.

Fingernails are bitten.

Dials are adjusted.

Lips are chewed.

Suddenly, over the stereo—I hear something. It's so soft, I wonder if I'm just imagining it. It's kinda like when you hold a seashell to your ear and you hear the ocean. But it gets louder. . . .

I spin around in the passenger seat. In the back of Big Mama, I see Dirk's lips moving and his face is stiff with pain.

His eyes are shut so tight it's like they're Krazy-Glued.

Quint adjusts the satellite, tilting it, and Dirk starts speaking louder and faster. It's incredible: these words are the direct thoughts of an entire interconnected horde of zombies—and they're being blasted into his brain and shot out through our stereo!

Quint adjusts the satellite once more and I crank the volume on the stereo. Dirk's in the back, spewing a strange stream of words.

You ever wonder what zombies think? I can tell you. . . . There's a lot about eating. Eating the sort of stuff nobody wants to hear about. Maybe sometime, after I've had enough ginger ale, I'll tell ya.

But there are other things, too.

A jumbled mess of words: *"Move. Go. Speaking. Tail. Now."*

And then—

"Rolling. Sliding."

Each word out of Dirk's mouth is spoken in a slightly different voice. It's him talking, for sure—but he's channeling the zombies.

Then he says two more words—and as he says them, his eyes flash open.

"WATER. MONSTER."

I gasp with realization: "The Scrapken! It's watching the zombies! And the zombies see The Scrapken!"

"Left! To the pier!" I shout as I stab at the map. June spins the wheel, and we slide out onto the avenue. Then we're speeding across town, flying up the hill past the library.

And on the way back down the hill, I see it.

It's a blip in the distance.

Miles away.

But it's there.

The Tendrill. It surges along like a branchy, viney Ferris wheel off its hinges.

If I squint hard enough, I can see the zombies. Every zombie from the farm, dotting the Tendrill. Like sprinkles on an ice cream cone.

Like the sprinkles scattering in the air as Bardle fell.

"Dirk," I say, jerking my head back. "Dirk, you did it. You can take the helmet off."

Quint immediately reverses it. The helmet bangs across the truck bed as Dirk rolls over onto his side. Beads of sweat trickle down his face and he gulps air. . . .

I think I'd like to nap now.

You're done, friend.

You won't have to do that again.

Dirk puts his hand on Quint's shoulder. He mumbles something like, "Thanks, bud."

"Well, we found it," June says. Her fingers are tight on the wheel as she watches the Tendrill. "Now what?"

"Now we get those zombies back," I say.

"It's *a lot* of zombies . . ." Quint says.

I nod. "And we're gonna need *a lot* of help."

With that, I reach my hand out the window, yank the spark on a firework—and it soars into the sky, exploding high above us with a—

SKA-BOOM!

"*Battle Royale?*" June says, smirking.

"Skaelka loves games," I say. "And I bet she'll be happy to bring some of her pals. . . ."

Ahead of us, the Tendrill surges and morphs as it slides along. I get a hollow, dark feeling in my stomach—it's a nightmare come to life.

June stomps on the gas and Big Mama zooms forward. Soon, we're close enough that I can see Thrull, atop the surging Tendrill like he's riding a tidal wave.

We lock eyes. And he smiles.

"June, watch out!" I suddenly shout, but I realize a moment too late. . . .

KA-SCHLURP!

Vines erupt from the backside of the Tendrill like monstrous party streamers. They reach beneath Big Mama, and there's a tremendously loud *shattering—*

Big Mama's gutted! The engine is torn open—and half of the truck's bottom falls away. Looking down, I see the wooden boardwalk racing by below us.

"My mom's gonna kill me . . ." Quint groans.

June jerks the wheel to avoid a Popsicle stand ahead, and the truck is spinning to a stop.

The Tendrill and Thrull are getting away!

Then I hear it. Looking back, I see them. . . .

Skaelka and the Carapace cavalry.

chapter
twenty-five

Dozens of crab-creatures wearing vehicular shells stampede toward us. Hundreds of neon green goo-slime canisters glow like fireflies. Skaelka's leading the charge in her own souped-up Carapace.

"We'll catch a ride with these dudes!" I say.

But Skaelka must have a different idea, because she's not slowing down. Instead, she ducks inside the Carapace and—

FLING!

The vehicle shell flips off—and we see the body beneath it. It's slimy and crab-like. Skaelka lies atop it, holding tight, as the Carapace's tiny, agile legs scurry forward at breakneck speed.

June looks out the back window. "Is Skaelka gonna stop, or . . . ?"

"NOT STOPPING!" Skaelka shouts. "BATTLE WAITS FOR NO MONSTER!"

Just moments before hitting us, the Carapace dips its head and gets close to the ground. Skaelka leans forward, hugging the creature tight.

"Brace yourselves!" I shout.

The Carapace slips beneath Big Mama, lifting it up. June dives into the backseat as Skaelka pops up, pulling herself through the twisted metal and into the driver's seat.

"FOLLOW THAT TENDRILL!" Quint barks, pointing ahead.

Skaelka steers Big Mama down the boardwalk, dodging rubble and jutting wooden planks. She has a crazed grin on her face as she spins the wheel back and forth.

"Um, Skaelka," I ask, leaning forward. "The wheel doesn't actually *do* anything, right? The car is just a shell."

"The wheel is only for looking cool," she replies. "But the pedals give us speed!"

I glance down—Big Mama has no *floor*—it's like something from *The Flintstones*. Skaelka stomps her foot on the pedal, pushing it down into the creature's fleshy back. The Carapace YELPS and speeds forward. . . .

"Well, that works," June says.

Up ahead, Thrull is watching. He scowls and swings his war hammer, bringing it crashing into a huge **HONKY-TONK HAMBURGERS** sign and—

SMASH!

It pounds the boardwalk, metal shattering, giant plastic burger exploding!

"We're gonna hit it!" I shout, but Skaelka *jerks* the gear shift, stomps the gas pedal, and—

We sail over the rubble, then—*WHOOMP!*

We hit the ground hard, and the Carapace's lower body picks up little pieces of splintered wood, which, *man*—that has *gotta* hurt, but it presses forward, catching up to the Tendrill.

"I need to get up there," I say.

"OK, time to get our zombies back . . ."
I say in my coolest action hero voice, 'cause I'm
about to do cool action hero stuff—

YANK!

Thrull's tail-arm grabs hold of me, and I'm
plucked from the passenger seat so hard that I
actually tear *through* the seat belt. I spin in the
air and flop down the mossy green Tendrill.

The zombies are all embedded within the
Tendrill's pulsating, moving form. One gnarled
hand reaches out for me as I scramble to my feet.

"Hello, Jack."

Thrull strides easily across the Tendrill's

257

surface. The vines gently grip his boots with each step, keeping him steady. Like his own personal red carpet.

The war hammer's other-dimensional steel glints in the light. . . .

I DID MUCH THINKING, DOWN THERE, WHILE I HEALED.

DO YOU KNOW WHAT I LEARNED?

I raise my eyes, meeting Thrull's square on. "Y'know, Thrull," I say. "Usually, I'd respond with some lousy attempt at quippy humor. But not now. I don't care what you learned, and I *really* don't care what you think—"

The only thing I care about is that you killed my friend.

My grip tightens around the Slicer as I unsheathe it—and Thrull laughs. Not exactly the reaction you want when making a dramatic grab for your weapon. He smirks and—*KA-SNAP!*

Thrull's tail-arm whips forward, like it's a *Mortal Kombat* thing. I half expect him to shout, "*Get over here!*" in a Scorpion voice. The tail-arm wraps around me, anaconda tight.

"Bardle stood in my way," he says. "And *nothing* can stand in my way. Because what I learned in that cavern is . . ."

Over the roar of the Tendrill and Thrull's evil-dude monologue, I hear June's voice. She's barking orders into the truck's old police radio mic. Big Mama's external speakers blare:

"MONSTER BUDDIES! FIRE THE GOO-SLIME! STOP THAT TENDRILL!"

From every car, every open window, every sunroof comes a blistering assault of Quint's goo-slime weaponry—

The Tendrill shudders and shakes. Thrull glances down—and in his distracted state, his tail-arm's grip loosens. I use the opportunity to try to wriggle my gloved hand free and escape the tail's hold.

But Thrull snarls, and the tail tightens again. "Jack, I cannot let you go free. Your blade, the hand—you are growing, evolving. . . ."

"Yeah, well, just wait until I get my big growth spurt," I say.

And with that, Thrull raises his war hammer. OK, this was fun and all, but I need to escape. *NOW*. I push and shove at the tail-arm with my half-free gloved hand. What happens next is legit BANANAS. My gloved hand *sinks* into the tail-arm and—

BZZZT!!

The same electric pulse I felt back in the ice cream shop, with Bardle.

Thrull feels it, too. I see a flash of confusion cross his face. "What is . . . ?"

It's not magic, it's not the Force or some sort of vision—this dark other-dimension energy is real, and it's inside the tail. A big mass of it courses through every molecule of the tail's fleshy skin. Just like it coursed through the Louisville Slicer at the ABC Theater.

The glove is pumping like a beating heart, its many suckers slurping. It's like it's *thirsty* for dark energy, and it's *drawing* it from the tail.

I think about Bardle's words right before he died. *"The decision . . . is now . . . in your hands. . . ."*

And I allow myself the briefest moment to smile—because with Bardle's final breath, he left me a message. Only he didn't mean *hands*, plural—but one *hand*.

"Thrull," I say. *"My* hand. And this thing that covers it. It's gonna *end you*."

Thrull releases a swift, guttural grunt. He attempts to pull away, but the glove has suctioned onto his arm with unbreakable force. I smile as my hand squeezes tighter around the tail, the suckers pulling on it like a vacuum.

The rat tail's skin begins to bubble. It's being pulled *into* the glove.

And now the full meaning of Bardle's words hits me.

"The decision . . . is now . . . in your hands. . . ."

The decision. It's my choice whether to take the power of the tail as my own.

My heart *should* be pounding and my mind *should* be racing, pinballing back and forth between TAKE IT and DON'T TAKE IT—

But it's not.

It's not much of a decision at all.

Right now, it's not about how big the responsibility feels. When Bardle thought I wasn't committed, he showed me that horrible image—the simulation of what could be. But it made my task feel so overwhelming that I wanted to cower from it.

I only successfully controlled the zombies when I focused on what makes this fight personal: *my friends*.

And that's what I do now.

The goo-slime attack continues with June at the helm: a series of BOOMs and SPLATs. And each BOOM seems to represent something deeper—what's really at stake.

If I don't do this, then my friends' happiness and hopes will be crushed. Their suffering and sadness will have been for nothing.

The thought only makes me squeeze tighter.

The tail-arm's leathery skin turns an inky black color—the same shade as the smoky energy that streaks off the Slicer.

The glove bubbles and grows. I smell burning and I see the last bit of energy extracted from the tail. After the process is complete, Thrull's left with a long, winding, skeletal appendage.

I've never seen Thrull less than 100 percent intimidating, so it takes me a second to realize he looks *defeated*.

But then he looks down.

And so do I.

A few of Evie's action figures—the bits of plastic that were embedded in Ghazt's tail—stick out from the tail bone like odd little spikes.

Thrull reaches out and touches them. I don't know what it is about them—but they cause a foul, unnerving grin to cross his face.

He opens his mouth, but the only words that come out are—

"HIT IT AGAIN!"

It's June, below, in Big Mama. My friends unleash another epic goo-slime blast, and—

The Tendrill rattles and quakes! It's melting, crumbling, collapsing beneath our feet. It's nearly destroyed.

Just one final blast.

That's when I spot Dirk and Quint, together in Big Mama's truck bed. A sheet is yanked away, flung into the air, revealing the *biggest* loot crate of all. . . .

The final volley of goo-slime is indescribable. The attack comes from all vantage points— exploding, blasting. The Tendrill thrashes—and its pained howl emanates from every inch of it. "Jack, go!" Quint shouts.

I throw a final glance at Thrull and shout— "Peace! Out! DOOF! WAD!"

I jump, just as I hear the cannon erupt. I sail through the air, then—"Gotcha!" Wez shouts.

"Thanks!" I holler. "Sorry we whooped you back at Battle Royale!"

I WILL HAVE MY REVENGE LATER. FOR NOW: I'LL SET YOU DOWN SAFELY!

The Tendrill is breaking down. Goo-slime clings to its branches and vines, turning them gray and brittle. They crack and snap like nuclear Rice Krispies.

The Tendrill's body arcs and its maw lurches upward, howling at the sky like a full-moon werewolf. Then—

KRAKA-SMASH!

The Tendrill SMASHES to the ground with earth-rattling force, rolling over on its side before going completely still.

The Vine-Thingies dissolve into something like green-orange ash, filling the air like a sandstorm. Then a sudden gust of wind, and— gone. The Tendrill has vanished.

The zombies are scattered across the road. They wobble to their feet. Goo-slime drips off them like dog slobber. Zombies are goo-slime resilient—good to know!

Amidst the fading, dissipating ash is Thrull. He stands bolt upright—you'd never guess that his cosmic transportation vessel just exploded out from underneath him. . . .

Thrull eyes me through the swirling ash.

At his side, the rat-tail appendage looks like a terrible skeleton whip. I stare at him—and at the many zombies between us. . . .

Something about this epic moment makes me think of Evie; just a few weeks ago, these same zombies were in the bowling alley—part of her and Ghazt's army.

And now? Ghazt's nowhere to be found, Thrull went rogue, and I'm suddenly the one with the zombie-controlling power she craved. . . .

The end of the world, man—never know what to expect! And now Evie knows that just as well as I do.

But Evie's not my concern right now. What matters is my friends—and the decision I have to make.

One last time, Bardle's words enter my consciousness: *It is your choice, Jack. But it is a tremendous burden. And for that, I am so very sorry. . . .*

I think, *Don't be sorry, dude.* I've made up my mind. Here goes nothin'.

chapter twenty-six

I reach my gloved hand back and draw the Slicer. The dark energy—that ebony ink—begins draining out of the glove and snakes up the Slicer's handle with a *SCHLURRRP*.

It seeps into the Slicer's every splinter, sliver, fracture, and fissure. It's joining with the dark, awful power already contained within it until, at last, the entire blade is the color of midnight. . . .

"Thrull," I say. "These zombies—your army—belong to ME now!" I swing the Slicer around, toward the zombies, and a chalky charcoal arc hangs in the air. My gloved hand throbs as the final bit of energy is absorbed into the bat, and—

Zombies are yanked toward me with magnetic force. They lean forward at an angle, feet dragging, just barely skimming the ground. They move so fast that I smell burning rubber from the ones still wearing shoes.

In half a second, all of them are gathered behind me.

Thrull can only watch.

The tip of his skeletal arm slowly grazes the ground. The arm lifts, and Thrull softly runs his hand over it.

Thrull looks up, a cryptic smile on his face as his hand continues to trace over the skeletal appendage. And the action figures embedded in it.

"This is so very far from over. The Tower *will* be built—though I may enlist a different kind of army," he says. He taps the skeletal tail, then smiles. "I suggest you get used to the sight of bones, Jack. . . ."

He lifts his war hammer, sets it over his shoulder, and makes a medium-dramatic exit. The skeletal arm drags behind him, until he snaps it up. A few tiny bits of remaining Vine-Thingies gather around him, following like gooey little snails. . . .

My friends come closer, but I take a hesitant step back.

"Guys, please," I say, throwing up my hand, all dramatic. "I have changed. . . . I . . . I am different now. I am no longer the Jack you know. I am . . . *more*."

I hoist the blade over my head.

"I must go now," I say. My face is somber. "I must learn the limits of these powers. It is my quest—my quest alone. And where I go, you cannot follow."

June's mouth hangs open. Quint is frozen. Dirk is quiet. I hang my head for a moment, and when I lift it up again—

I'm giggling so hard I snort. "Just messing with you! But, yeah, that *was* legit crazy. I'm still me, though, and if I ever hear anyone say they are 'close personal friends of the hero' again I will FLIP."

"Good," June says. "I like regular ol' Jack."

Suddenly, Quint points. "Jack! Your hand! The glove!"

I hear scattered whispers among the monsters. "Whoa," says Dirk.

I lift my hand, twisting it, looking at it from all angles.

The Scrapken flesh has smoothed over. It crosses over that weird tight fleshy part between the thumb and the pointer finger, then back around, over my palm, where it fused together.

It's tight, but not uncomfortable. Still wet. Still changing.

It's not a glove anymore.

It appears to be . . . permanent.

Quint's right. This thing ain't comin' off. The power is mine—and this is part of it . . . permanently. . . .

Sure, I was joking before—but I *have* changed. And I don't think there's any going back.

My stomach gurgles. I suddenly want to barf.

Did I make a mistake? My knees go wobbly, but then I feel a hand on my shoulder. It's June.

"Hey, Jack," she says. "That weird hand thing of yours. You know what it means, right?"

"No," I say quietly.

And she grins.

We can do the best fist bumps now, duder!

BOOP!

In a flash—the pukey feeling is gone, and I think things are gonna be OK.

"This warm-hearted sharing of humor makes Skaelka's skin crawl," Skaelka says. "Skaelka is leaving before it escalates to hugging. Monsters, follow me—pizza at Joe's! We will eat until our stomachs are round—in honor of Bardle!"

The monsters climb up into their Carapace cars and take off for home.

"Hold up, let me get this straight," Dirk says after they've gone. "June has a Leatherman multi-tool blaster on her arm, Thrull's got a whole SKELETON WHIP ARM. And now, Jack— you have this—this—this sucker *glove*."

"Good point," Quint says. "I would like a special hand. Are we all getting special hands?"

"If we're all getting special hands," Dirk says, "I want a chainsaw—now that would be *groovy*."

"On second thought, I need no special hand," Quint says, "but I do have a concept for a monster-battling tool of my own. Although, June—I will need your assistance. But, oh, I am excited just thinking about it. . . ."

I smile as we walk.

I love these guys.

chapter
twenty-seven

We lead the zombies to the farm, depositing them there—even though Warg is nowhere in sight.

It's only when we get to the crumbled remains of Dandy-Lions ice cream parlor that we find her carrying Bardle in her arms. The other monsters are back at Joe's, celebrating our victory. They do not mourn Bardle.

Only Warg does.

She is different from the other monsters. She doesn't quite fit in. And man, it's a weird reminder that being different and not fitting in—that's *good* sometimes.

"What will you do with Bardle?" I ask.

"We have our own customs," Warg says. "You need not know any more than that."

The next few days are a weird, hazy blur of *nothing*. I read comics that I've already read a thousand times—just looking for the comfort of familiarity.

Quint immediately gets back to work—probably drawing up a blueprint of his cool new weapon.

June curls up on the couch, watching her parents' names scroll down the cracked TV on a loop, for hours and hours a day.

And Dirk.

Dirk is quiet.

It's almost three days after our big battle when Quint comes flying out of his lab. He's carrying the football helmet. "Dirk!" he says. "Put this on! No delaying!"

Dirk's flopped out on a beanbag in the corner. "Whaddya want me to find this time?"

Quint shakes his head and says softly, "I want you to find the peace and quiet you deserve, friend."

"That's so corny, bro," Dirk says. But he smiles, sits up, and cracks his neck. Quint reaches up to place the helmet on Dirk's head. "I made some modifications," Quint says. "The helmet now *blocks* intrusive zombie thoughts.

I've added custom settings, too, so this knob here, on the side, allows the zombie thoughts back *in*, if you like."

For a split second, it looks like Dirk might cry. "You mean . . . ?"

"Yep." Quint nods, all proud. "Zombie-*cancelling* helmet."

I feel better already. . . .

It's a whole week later, and I'm itching to play video games—but June's still watching the names on the screen. I'll be honest, she totally monopolizes the TV—but I guess these are special circumstances.

But it's the siren call of the video game that causes me to grab a spare console and head out to the football field early one morning. I fire up the system—no *Battle Royale* today, just some retro, single-player side-scroller stuff.

Rover curls up on the grass, and I lean back against him—sinking into his warm, soft belly fur. I grab the controller and realize this new Squishy Mitten of Power is going to take some getting used to on the video game front. And it also needs a name that isn't the Squishy Mitten of Power.

I play for hours. Happy to have knocked Thrull back—big-time.

I play for so long that I actually drift off midgame—soothed by the sounds of 16-bit tunes.

But then Quint's shaking me awake. He's with Warg and Dirk. I rub my eyes, confused.

They have Evie's book: *Interdimensional Terrors: A History of the Cabal of the Cosmic*.

"Uh, hey, guys," I say, wiping drool from my chin. "What's up?"

Quint taps the book. "After all my research on the tail, I *needed* to know how Bardle was able to give you the ability to absorb the tail's energy. I kept thinking there had to be a scientific reason. So, I consulted the book."

"And what did you find?" I ask.

"Nothing good," Quint says. "Jack, when you pulled the power from the tail—did the tail appear to *retain* any of that power?"

"No. It was all bone. There was none of that inky, oily stuff left."

"Are you *certain*?" Warg asks.

"I think so! I mean, it was kind of a high-stress situation—I wasn't exactly taking notes. Why?"

The book says that if anything remains after a "transference"—any totems or talismans—then some cosmic power can remain. . . .

BUT THAT POWER WILL BE SLIGHTLY ALTERED—SIMILAR, BUT NOT ENTIRELY THE SAME. . . .

Oh no . . .

Evie's action figures . . .

I think back to what Thrull said to me, at the end. "Get used to the sight of bones. . . ."

I thought it was just a general sort of threat—like, y'know, he'd be doing mean-guy stuff that would turn me into a pile of bones or something.

But he meant it in an entirely different way. Because Thrull and I—our eyes both locked on those melted action figures—the ones that remained inside the tail-arm.

And if they retain power—then . . .

Thrull said, "A different kind of army."

And I suddenly grab the book from Quint's hand. I'm flipping through it—hoping that I'm wrong. Hoping that it's not true.

But then I see it.

Right there.

In the book.

Ancient drawings that show not *zombies*—but *skeletal soldiers*.

"Oh no . . ." I whisper.

And I shut my eyes.

What happens next is all in my head— I know that. But it feels like what I see is— unfortunately for us—a vision of what's to come. . . .

MERP!

Acknowledgments

As always, so thankful to Douglas Holgate for seeing beyond my mutterings and harebrained ideas and creating a world that is fun, beautiful, inviting, and so funny and so perfectly scary. Dana Leydig, my patient (x19), encouraging, and inspiring editor for making magic of a mess—thank you! Jim Hoover, for seeing this whole thing perfectly; your endless dedication and understanding means the (end of the) world to me. Jennifer Dee, my publicist who makes the most remarkable things happen. To Abigail Powers, Janet Pascal, Krista Ahlberg, and Marinda Valenti—thanks for saving me from embarrassment and making certain my writing arrives (mostly) typo free and plot-hole free to the readers.

Erin Berger, Emily Romero, Carmela
Iaria, Christina Colangelo, Felicity Vallence,
Sarah Moses, Kim Ryan, Helen Boomer, Kara
Brammer, Michael Hetrick, Alex Garber, and
absolutely everyone in Viking's marketing and
publicity department—thank you for listening,
believing, and wowing readers and booksellers
with your unmatched creativity. And of course,
Ken Wright, for always being there, from the
very first moment. For Robin Hoffman and all
the wonderful people at Scholastic, for your
endless support and dedication, for bringing
books to kids. Dan Lazar, at Writers House,
for making all this (and so much else) happen.
Cecilia de la Campa and Alessandra Birch, for
the thrill of taking Jack, June, Quint, and Dirk
across the world. Torie Doherty-Munro, for
hand-holding and patience. And Addison Duffy
and Kassie Evashevski, for taking this where
I dreamed. Matt Berkowitz and Scott Peterson
for "getting" it and always getting it better.
Josh Pruett and Haley Mancini for wonderful
feedback along the way. And my parents and my
sister—I love you!

MAX BRALLIER!

is the *New York Times* and *USA Today* bestselling author of more than thirty books for children and adults. His books and series include the Last Kids on Earth, Eerie Elementary, Mister Shivers, Galactic Hot Dogs, and Can YOU Survive the Zombie Apocalypse? Max lives in New York City with his wife, Alyse, who is way too good for him, and his daughter, Lila, who is simply the best.

The author building his own tree house as a kiddo.

DOUGLAS HOLGATE!

has been a freelance comic book artist and illustrator based in Melbourne, Australia, for more than ten years. He's illustrated books for publishers such as HarperCollins, Penguin Random House, Hachette, and Simon & Schuster, including the Planet Tad series, Cheesie Mack, Case File 13, and *Zoo Sleepover*.

Douglas has illustrated comics for Image, Dynamite, Abrams, and Penguin Random House. He's currently working on the self-published series Maralinga, which received grant funding from the Australian Society of Authors and the Victorian Council for the Arts, as well as the all-ages graphic novel *Clem Hetherington and the Ironwood Race*, published by Scholastic Graphix, both co-created with writer Jen Breach.